Jim Thompson (1906–1977) was born in Anadarko, Oklahoma. Among his many novels are *The Killer Inside Me*, *The Grifters*, *Pop. 1280* and *After Dark, My Sweet*. He also wrote two screenplays (for the Stanley Kubrick films *The Killing* and *Paths of Glory*). *The Getaway* has been filmed twice, in 1972 (by Sam Peckinpah) and 1994.

By Jim Thompson

Jim Thompson

The Grifters

ORION

An Orion paperback

First published in Great Britain in 2003
by Orion
This paperback edition published in 2005
by Orion Books Ltd,
Orion House, 5 Upper St Martin's Lane,
London WC2H 9EA

First published in the United States of America in 1963
by Regency
in somewhat different form

10 9 8 7 6 5 4 3 2 1

A CIP catalogue record for this book is available
from the British Library.

ISBN 0 75286 428 9

Typeset at SetSystems Ltd, Saffron Walden, Essex
Printed and bound in Great Britain by
Clays Ltd, St Ives plc

www.orionbooks.co.uk

As Roy Dillon stumbled out of the shop his face was a sickish green, and each breath he drew was an incredible agony. A hard blow in the guts can do that to a man, and Dillon had gotten a hard one. Not with a fist, which would have been bad enough, but from the butt-end of a heavy club.

Somehow, he got back to his car and managed to slide into the seat. But that was all he could manage. He moaned as the change in posture cramped his stomach muscles; then, with a strangled gasp, he leaned out the window.

Several cars passed as he spewed vomit into the street, their occupants grinning, frowning sympathetically, or averting their eyes in disgust. But Roy Dillon was too sick to notice or to care if he had. When at last his stomach was empty, he felt better, though still not well enough to drive. By then, however, a prowl car had pulled up behind him – a sheriff's car, since he was in the county rather than city of Los Angeles – and a brown-clad deputy was inviting him to step out to the walk.

Dillon shakily obeyed.

'One too many, mister?'

'What?'

'Never mind.' The cop had already noticed the absence of liquor breath. 'Let's see your driver's license.'

Dillon showed it to him, also displaying, with seeming inadvertence, an assortment of credit cards. Suspicion washed off the cop's face, giving way to concern.

'You seem pretty sick, Mr Dillon. Any idea what caused it?'

'My lunch, I guess. I know I should know better, but I had a chicken-salad sandwich – and it didn't taste quite right when I was eating it – but . . .' He let his voice trail away, smiling a shy, rueful smile.

'Mmm-hmm!' The cop nodded grimly. 'That stuff will do it to you. Well' – a shrewd up-and-down look – 'you all right, now? Want us to take you to a doctor?'

'Oh, no. I'm fine.'

'We got a first-aid man over to the substation. No trouble to run you over there.'

Roy declined, pleasantly but firmly. Any prolonged contact with the cops would result in a record, and any kind of record was at best a nuisance. So far he had none; the scrapes which the grift had led him into had not led him to the cops. And he meant to keep it that way.

The deputy went back to the prowl car, and he and his partner drove off. Roy waved a smiling farewell to them and got back into his own car. Gingerly, wincing a little, he got a cigarette lit. Then, convinced that the last of the vomiting was over, he forced himself to lean back against the cushions.

He was in a suburb of Los Angeles, one of the many which resist incorporation despite their interdependence and the lack of visible boundaries. From here it was almost a thirty-mile drive back into the city, a very long thirty miles at this hour of the day. He needed to be in better shape than he was, to rest a while, before bucking the outbound tide of evening traffic. More important, he needed to reconstruct the details of his recent disaster, while they still remained fresh in his mind.

He closed his eyes for a moment. He opened them again, focusing them on the changing lights of the nearby traffic standard. And suddenly, without moving from the car – without physically moving from it – he was back inside the shop again. Sipping a limeade at the fountain, while he casually studied his surroundings.

It was little different from a thousand small shops in Los Angeles, establishments with an abbreviated soda fountain, a showcase or two of cigars, cigarettes, and candy, and overflowing racks of magazines, paperback books, and greeting cards. In the East, such shops were referred to as stationers' or candy stores. Here they were usually called confectionaries or simply fountains.

Dillon was the only customer in the place. The one other person present was the clerk, a large, lumpy-looking youth of perhaps nineteen or twenty. As Dillon finished his drink, he noted the boy's manner as he tapped ice down around the freezer containers, working with a paradoxical mixture of diligence and indifference. He knew exactly what needed to be done, his expression said, and to hell with doing a bit more than that. Nothing for show, nothing to impress anyone. The boss's son, Dillon decided, putting down his glass and sliding off the stool. He sauntered up toward the cash register, and the youth laid down the sawed-off ball bat with which he had been tamping. Then, wiping his hands on his apron, he also moved up to the register.

'Ten cents,' he said.

'And a package of those mints, too.'

'Twenty cents.'

'Twenty cents, hmm?' Roy began to fumble through his pockets, while the clerk fidgeted impatiently. 'Now, I know I've got some change here. Bound to have. I wonder where the devil . . .'

Exasperatedly, he shook his head and drew out his wallet. 'I'm sorry. Mind cashing a twenty?'

The clerk almost snatched the bill from his hand. He slapped the bill down on the cash register ledge and counted out the change from the drawer. Dillon absently picked it up, continuing his fumbling search of his pockets.

'Now, doesn't that get you? I mean, you know darned well you've got something, but – ' He broke off, eyes widening with a pleased smile. 'There it is – two dimes! Just give me back my twenty, will you?'

The clerk grabbed the dimes from him, and tossed back the bill. Dillon turned casually toward the door, pausing, on the way out, for a disinterested glance at the magazine display.

Thus, for the tenth time that day, he had worked the *twenties*, one of the three standard gimmicks of the short con grift. The other two are the *smack* and the *tat*, usually good for bigger scores but not nearly so swift nor safe. Some marks fall for the twenties repeatedly, without ever tipping.

Dillon didn't see the clerk come around the counter. The guy was just there, all of a sudden, a pouty snarl on his face, swinging the sawed-off bat like a battering ram.

'Dirty crook,' he whinnied angrily. 'Dirty crooks keep cheatin' me and cheatin' me, an' Papa cusses me out for it!'

The butt of the bat landed in Dillon's stomach. Even the clerk was startled by its effect. 'Now, you can't blame me, mister,' he stammered. 'You were askin' for it. I – I give you change for twenty dollars, an' then you have me give the twenty back, an' – an'' – his self-righteousness began to crumble. 'N-now, you k-know you did, m-mister.'

Roy could think of nothing but his agony. He turned swimming eyes on the clerk, eyes flooded with pain-filled puzzlement. The look completely demolished the youth.

'It w-was j-just a mistake, mister. Y-you made a m-mistake, an' I m-made a m-m-mistake an' – mister!' He backed away, terrified. 'D-don't look at me like that!'

'You killed me,' Dillon gasped. 'You killed me, you rotten bastard!'

'Nah! P-please don't say t-that, mister!'

'I'm dying,' Dillon gasped. And, then, somehow, he had gotten out of the place.

And now, seated in his car and re-examining the incident, he could see no reason to fault himself, no flaw in his technique. It was just bad luck. He'd simply caught a goof, and goofs couldn't be figured.

He was right about that. And he'd been right about something else, although he didn't know it.

As he drove back to Los Angeles, constantly braking and speeding up in the thickening traffic, repeatedly stopping and starting – with every passing minute, he was dying.

Death might be forestalled if he took proper care of himself. Otherwise, he had no more than three days to live.

2

Roy Dillon's mother was from a family of backwoods white trash. She was thirteen when she married a thirty-year-old railroad worker, and not quite fourteen when she gave birth to Roy. A month or so after his birth, her husband suffered an accident which made her a widow. Thanks to the circumstances of its happening, it also made her well-off by the community's standards. A whole two hundred dollars a month to spend on herself. Which was right where she meant to spend it.

Her family, on whom she promptly dumped Roy, had other ideas. They kept the boy for three years, occasionally managing to wheedle a few dollars from their daughter. Then, one day, her father appeared in town, bearing Roy under one arm and swinging a horsewhip with the other. And he proceeded to demonstrate his lifelong theory that a gal never got too old to whip.

Since Lilly Dillon's character had been molded long before, it was little changed by the thrashing. But she did keep Roy, having no choice in the matter, and frightened by her father's grim promises to keep an eye on her, she moved out of his reach.

Settling down in Baltimore, she found lucrative and

6

undemanding employment as a B-girl. Or, more accurately, it was undemanding as far as she was concerned. Lilly Dillon wasn't putting out for anyone; not, at least, for a few bucks or drinks. Her nominal heartlessness often disgruntled the customers, but it drew the favorable attention of her employers. After all, the world was full of bimbos, tramps who could be had for a grin or a gin. But a smart kid, a doll who not only had looks and class, but was also *smart* – well, that kind of kid you could use.

They used her, in increasingly responsible capacities. As a managing hostess, as a recruiter for a chain of establishments, as a spotter of sticky-fingered and bungling employees; as courier, liaison officer, finger-woman; as a collector and disburser. And so on up the ladder . . . or should one say down it? The money poured in, but little of the shower settled on her son.

She wanted to pack him off to boarding school, only drawing back, indignantly, when the charges were quoted to her. A couple thousand dollars a year, plus a lot of extras, and just for taking care of a kid! Just for keeping a kid out of trouble! Why, for that much money she could buy a nice mink jacket.

They must think she was a sucker, she decided. Nuisance that he was, she'd just look after Roy herself. And he'd darned well keep out of trouble or she'd skin him alive.

She was, of course, imbued with certain ineradicable instincts, eroded and atrophied though they were; so she had her rare moments of conscience. Also, certain things had to be done, for the sake of appearances: to stifle charges of neglect and the unpleasantness pursuant thereto. In either case, obviously, and as Roy instinctively knew, whatever she did was for herself, out of fear or as a salve for her conscience.

Generally, her attitude was that of a selfish older sister to an annoying little brother. They quarreled with each other. She delighted in gobbling down his share of some treat, while he danced about her in helpless rage.

'You're mean! Just a dirty old pig, that's all!'

'Don't you call me names, you snot!' – striking at him. 'I'll learn you!'

'Learn me, learn me! Don't even have enough sense to say teach!'

'I do, too! I did say teach!'

He was an excellent student in school, and exceptionally well-behaved. Learning came easily for him, and good behavior seemed simply a matter of common sense. Why risk trouble when it didn't make you anything? Why be profitlessly detained after school when you could be out hustling newspapers or running errands or caddying? Time was money, and money was what made the world go around.

As the smartest and best-behaved boy in his classes, he naturally drew the displeasure of the other kind. But no matter how cruelly or frequently he was attacked, Lilly offered only sardonic condolence.

'Only one arm?' she would say, if he exhibited a twisted and swollen arm.

Or if a tooth had been knocked out, 'Only one tooth?'

And when he received an overall mauling, with dire threats of worse to come, 'Well, what are you kicking about? They may kill you, but they can't eat you.'

Oddly enough, he found a certain comfort in her back-handed remarks. On the surface they were worse than nothing, merely insult added to injury, but beneath them lay a chilling and callous logic. A fatalistic do-or-be-damned philosophy which could accommodate itself to anything but oblivion.

He had no liking for Lilly, but he came to admire her. She'd never given him anything but a hard time, which was about the extent of her generosity to anyone. But she'd done all right. She knew how to take care of herself.

She showed no soft spots until he was entering his teens, a handsome, wholesome-looking youth with coal-black hair and wide-set gray eyes. Then, to his secret amusement, he began to note a subtle change in her attitude, a softening of her voice when she spoke to him and a suppressed hunger in her eyes when she looked at him. And seeing her thus, knowing what was behind the change, he delighted in teasing her.

Was something wrong? Did she want him to clear out for a while and leave her alone?

'Oh, no, Roy. Really. I – I like being together with you.'

'Now, Lilly. You're just being polite. I'll get out of your way right now.'

'Please, h-honey . . .' Biting her lip at the unaccustomed endearment, a shamed flush spreading over her lovely features. 'Please stay with me. After all, I'm – I'm y-your m-mother.'

But she wasn't, remember? She'd always passed him off as her younger brother, and it was too late to change the story.

'I'll leave right now, Lilly. I know you want me to. You just don't want to hurt my feelings.'

He had matured early, as was natural enough. By the time he was seventeen-going-on-eighteen, the spring that he graduated from high school, he was as mature as a man in his twenties.

On the night of his graduation, he told Lilly that he was pulling out. For good.

'Pulling out . . . ?' She'd been expecting that, he guessed, but she wasn't resigned to it. 'B-but – but you can't! You've got to go to college.'

'Can't. No money.'

She laughed shakily, and called him silly; avoiding his eyes, refusing to be rejected as she must have known she would be.

'Of course, you have money! I've got plenty, and anything I have is yours. You –'

'"Anything I have is yours,"' Roy, eyes narrowed appreciably. 'That would make a good title for a song, Lilly.'

'You can go to one of the really good schools, Roy. Harvard or Yale, or some place like that. Your grades are certainly good enough, and with my money – our money . . .'

'Now, Lilly. You know you need the money for yourself. You always have.'

She flinched, as though he had struck her, and her face worked sickishly, and the trim size-nine suit seemed suddenly to hang on her: a cruel moral to a life that had gotten her everything and given her nothing. And for a moment, he almost relented. He almost pitied her.

And then she spoiled it all. She began to weep, to bawl like a child, which was a silly, stupid thing for Lilly Dillon to do; and to top off the ridiculous and embarrassing performance, she threw on the corn.

'D-don't be mean to me, Roy. Please, please don't. Y-you – you're b-breaking my heart . . .'

Roy laughed out loud. He couldn't restrain himself.

'Only one heart, Lilly?' he said.

Roy Dillon lived in a hotel called the Grosvenor-Carlton, a name which hinted at a grandeur that was wholly non-existent. It boasted one hundred rooms, one hundred baths, but it was purely a boast. Actually, there were only eighty rooms and thirty-five baths, and those included the hall baths and the two lobby restrooms which were not really baths at all.

It was a four-story affair with a white sandstone facade, and a small, terrazzo-floored lobby. The clerks were elderly pensioners, who were delighted to work for a minuscule salary and a free room. The Negro bellboy, whose badge of office was a discarded conductor's cap, also doubled as janitor, elevator operator, and all-around handyman. With such arrangements as these, the service left something to be desired. But, as the briskly jovial proprietor pointed out, anyone who was in a helluva hurry could hurry right on out to one of the Beverly Hills hotels, where he could doubtless get a nice little room for fifty bucks a day instead of the Grosvenor-Carlton's minimum of fifty a month.

Generally speaking, the Grosvenor-Carlton was little different than the numerous other 'family' and 'commercial' hotels which are strung out along West Seventh and Santa

Monica and other arterial streets of West Los Angeles; establishments catering to retired couples, and working men and women who required a close-in address. Mostly, these latter, single people, were men – clerks, white collar workers and the like – for the proprietor was strongly prejudiced against unattached women.

'Put it this way, Mr Dillon,' he said, during the course of their initial meeting. 'I rent to a woman, and she has to have a room with a bath. I insist on it, see, because otherwise she's got the hall bath tied up all the time, washing her goddamn hair and her clothes and every other damned thing she can think of. So the minimum for a room with a bath is seventeen a week – almost eighty bucks a month, just for a place to sleep and no cooking allowed. And just how many of these chicks make enough to pay eighty a month for a sleeping room and take all their meals in restaurants and buy clothes and a lot of frigging goo to smear on the faces that the good Lord gave 'em, and – and – You a God-fearing man, Mr Dillon?'

Roy nodded encouragingly; not for the world would he have interrupted the proprietor. People were his business, knowing them was. And the only way of knowing was to listen to them.

'Well, so am I. I and my late wife, goddamn – God rest her, we entered the church at the same time. That was thirty-seven years ago, down in Wichita Falls, Texas, where I had my first hotel. And that's where I began to learn about chicks. They just don't make the money for hotel livin', see, and there's only one way they can get it. By selling their stuff, you know; tapping them cute little piggy banks they all got. At first, they just do it now and then, just enough to make ends meet. But pretty soon they got the bank open twenty-four hours a day; why the hell not, is the way they see it. All they got to do is open up that cute little slot, and the money pours out; and it's no skin off their butts if they give a hotel a bad name.

'Oh, I tell you, Mr Dillon. I've hotelled all over this wonderful land of ours, and I'm telling you that hookers and hotellin' just don't mix. It's against God's laws, and it's against man's laws. You'd think the police would be too busy catching *real* criminals, instead of snooping around for hookers, but that's the way the gravy stains, as the saying is, and I don't fight it. An ounce of prevention, that's my motto. If you keep out the chicks, you keep out the hookers, and you've got a nice clean respectable place like this one, without a lot of cops hanging around. Why, if a cop comes in here now, I know he's a new man, and I tell him he'd better come back after he checks with headquarters. And he never comes back, Mr Dillon; he's damned well told that it ain't necessary, because this is a hotel not a hook shop.'

'I'm pleased to hear that, Mr Simms,' Roy said truthfully. 'I've always been very careful where I lived.'

'Right. A man's got to be,' Simms said. 'Now, let's see. You wanted a two-room suite, say, parlor, bedroom, and bath. Fact is, we don't have much demand for suites here. Got the suites split off into room with bath, and room without. But . . .'

He unlocked a door, and ushered his prospective tenant into a roomy bedroom, its high ceilings marking its prewar vintage. The connecting door opened into another room, a duplicate of the first except that it had no bath. This was the former parlor, and Simms assured Roy that it could be converted back into one in short order.

'Sure, we can take out this bedroom furniture. Move

back the parlor stuff in no time at all – desk, lounge, easy chairs, anything you want within reason. Some of the finest furniture you ever saw.'

Dillon said he would like to take a look at it, and Simms conducted him to the basement storeroom. It was by no means the finest he had ever seen, of course, but it was decent and comfortable; and he neither expected nor wanted anything truly fine. He had a certain image to maintain. A portrait of a young man who made rather a good living – just good, no better – and lived well within it.

He inquired the rental on the suite. Simms approached the issue circuitously, pointing out the twin necessities of maintaining a high-class clientele, for he would settle for nothing less, by God, and also making a profit, which was goddamn hard for a God-fearing man to do in these times.

'Why, some of these peasants we get in here, I mean that *try* to get in here, they'll fight you for a burned-out light globe. You just can't please 'em, know what I mean? It's like crackerjacks, you know, the more they get the more they want. But that's the way the cinnamon rolls, I guess, and like we used to say down in Wichita Falls, if you can't stand posts you better not dig holes. Uh, one hundred and twenty-five a month, Mr Dillon?'

'That sounds reasonable,' Roy smiled. 'I'll take it.'

'I'm sorry, Mr Dillon. I'd like to shave it a little for you; I ain't saying I *wouldn't* shave it for the right kind of tenant. If you'd guarantee, now to stay a minimum of three months, why – '

'Mr Simms,' said Roy.

' – why, I could make you a special rate. I'll lean over backward to – '

'Mr Simms,' Dillon said firmly. 'I'll take the place on a

year's lease. First and last month's rent in advance. And one hundred and twenty-five a month will be fine.'

'It – it will?' The proprietor was incredulous. 'You'll lease for a year at a hundred and twenty-five, and – and – '

'I will. I don't believe in moving around a lot. I make a profit in my business, and I expect others to make one in theirs.'

Simms gurgled. He gasped. His paunch wriggled in his pants, and his entire face, including the area which extended back into his balding head, reddened with pleasure. He was a shrewd and practiced student of human nature, he declared. He knew peasants when he saw them, and he knew gentlemen; he'd immediately spotted Roy Dillon as one of the latter.

'And you're smart,' he nodded wisely. 'You know it just ain't good business to chisel where you live. What the hell? What's the percentage in chiselling a hotel for a few bucks – people you're going to see every day – if it's going to make 'em a little down on you?'

'You're absolutely right,' Dillon said warmly.

Simms said he was damned tootin' he was right. Suppose, for example, that there was an inquiry about a guest of the peasant type. What could you honestly say about him anyway, beyond saying that he did live there and it was your Christian practice to say nothing about a man unless you could say something good? But if a *gentleman* was the subject of the inquiry, well, then, honesty compelled you to say so. He didn't simply *room* at the hotel, he *lived* there, a man of obvious character and substance who leased by the year and . . .

Dillon nodded and smiled, letting him ramble on. The Grosvenor-Carlton was the sixth hotel he'd visited since his arrival from Chicago. All had offered quarters which were equal to and as cheap or cheaper than those he had taken here. For there is a chronic glut of rooms in Los Angeles's smaller hotels. But he had found vaguely indefinable objections to all of them. They didn't *look* quite right. They didn't *feel* quite right. Only the Grosvenor-Carlton and Simms had had the right feel and look.

'. . . one more thing,' Simms was saying now. 'This is your home, see? Renting like you do, it's just the same as if you were in an apartment or house. It's your castle, like the law says, and if you should want to have a guest, you know, a lady guest, why you got a perfect right to.'

'Thank you for telling me,' Roy nodded gravely. 'I don't have anyone in mind at the moment, but I usually make friends wherever I go.'

'O' course. A fine-looking young fellow like you is bound to have lady friends, and I bet they got class too. None of these roundheels that crumb a place up just by walking through the lobby.'

'Never,' Dillon assured him. 'I'm very careful of the friends I make, Mr Simms. Particularly the lady friends.'

He was careful. During his four-year tenancy at the hotel he had had only one female visitor, a divorcee in her thirties, and everything about her – looks, dress, and manners – was abundantly satisfactory even to the discriminating Mr Simms. The only fault he could find with her was that she did not come often enough. For Moira Langtry was also discriminating. Given her own way, something that Dillon frequently refrained from giving her as a matter of policy, she wouldn't have come within a mile of the Grosvenor-Carlton. After all, she had a very nice apartment of her own, a place with one bedroom, two baths and a wet bar. If he really wanted to see her – and she was beginning to doubt that he did – why couldn't he come out there?

'Well, why can't you?' she said, as he sat up in bed phoning to her. 'It's no further for you than it is for me.'

'But you're so much younger, dear. A youthful female like you can afford to humor a doddering old man.'

'Flattery will get you nowhere, mister' – she was pleased. 'I'm five years older, and I feel every minute of it.'

Dillon grinned. *Five* years older? Hell, she was ten if she was a day. 'The fact is, I'm a little under the weather,' he explained. 'No, no, it's nothing contagious. I happened to trip over a chair the other night in the dark, and it gave me a nasty whack in the stomach.'

'Well . . . I guess I could come . . .'

'That's my girl. I'd hold my breath if I wasn't panting.'

'Mmm? Let's hear you.'

'Pant, pant,' he said.

'You poor thing,' she said. 'Moira'll hurry just as fast as she can.'

Apparently, she had been dressed to go out when he called, for she arrived in less than an hour. Or, perhaps, it only seemed that way. He had got up to unlock the door preparatory to her arrival, and returning to bed he had felt strangely tired and faint. So he had let his eyes drift shut, and when he opened them, a very little later seemingly, she was entering the room. Sweeping into it on her tiny, spike-heeled shoes; a billowing but compact bundle of woman with glossily black hair, and direct darkly-burning eyes.

She paused just inside the threshold for a moment, self-assured but suppliant. Posing like one of those arrogantly inviting mannequins. Then, she reached behind her, feeling for and finding the doorkey. And turning it with a soft click.

Roy forgot to wonder about her age.

She was old enough, was Moira Langtry.

She was young enough.

His silent approval spoke to her, and she gave a little twitch to her body, letting the ermine stole hang from one shoulder. Then, hips swaying delicately, she came slowly across the room; small chin outthrust; seemingly tugged forward by the bountiful imbalance within the small white blouse.

She stopped with her knees pressed against his bed, and looking upward he could see nothing but the tip of her nose above the contours of her breasts.

Raising a finger, he poked her in one then the other.

'You're hiding,' he said. 'Come out, come out, wherever you are.'

She sank gracefully to her knees, let her dark eyes burn into his face.

'You stink,' she said, tonelessly, the blouse shimmering with her words. 'I hate you.'

'The twins seem to be restless,' he said. 'Maybe we should put them to bed.'

'You know what I'm going to do? I'm going to smother you.'

He said, 'Death, where is thy sting?' and then he was necessarily voiceless for a while. After an incredibly soft, sweet-smelling eternity, he was allowed to come up for air. And he spoke to her in a whisper.

'You smell good, Moira. Like a bitch in a hothouse.'

'Darling. What a beautiful thing to say!'

'Maybe you don't smell good . . .'
'I do, too. You just said so.'
'It could be your clothes.'
'It's me! Want me to prove it to you?'
He did, and she did.

4

When he first settled in Los Angeles, Roy Dillon's interest in women was prudently confined by necessity. He was twenty-one, an oldish twenty-one. His urge toward the opposite sex was as strong as any man's; flourishing even stronger, perhaps, because of the successes that lay behind him. But he was carrying light, as the saying is. He had looked around extensively and carefully before choosing Los Angeles as a permanent base of operations, and his capital was now reduced to less than a thousand dollars.

That was a lot of money, of course. Unlike the big-con operator, whose elaborate scene-setting may involve as much as a hundred thousand dollars, the short-con grifter can run on peanuts. But Roy Dillon, while remaining loyal to the short con, was abandoning the normal scheme of things.

At twenty-one, he was weary of the hit-and-get. He knew that the constant 'getting' – jumping from one town to another before the heat got too hot – could absorb most of the hits, even of a thrifty man. So that he might work as hard and often as he safely could, and still wind up with the wolf nipping at the seat of his threadbare pants.

Roy had seen such men.

Once, on an excursion special out of Denver, he had run into a 'mob' of them, poor devils so depleted in capital that they had had to pool their resources.

They were working in a monte swindle. The dealer was cast as the 'wise guy,' whom the others were determined to take. While he turned his head to argue with the two shills – holding the three cards open on his palm – the roper had drawn a small mark on the top card, winking extravagantly at Roy.

'Take him, pal!' His stage whisper was ridiculously loud. 'Put down that big bill you got.'

'The fifty or the hundred?' Roy whispered back.

'The hundred! Hurry!'

'Could I bet five hundred?'

'Well, uh, naw. You just better make it a hundred to start.'

The dealer's conveniently outstretched hand was getting tired. The shills were running out of arguments to distract his attention. But Roy persisted with his cruel joke.

'How big is the marked card?'

'An ace, damnit! The other two are deuces! Now – '

'Does an ace beat deuces?'

'Does an – ! Hell, yes, damnit! Now, bet!'

The other passengers in the bar car were catching on, beginning to grin. Roy laboriously took out his wallet, and took out a C-note. The dealer counted out a crumpled mass of ones and fives. Then, he shuffled, palming the marked ace for a marked deuce, and switching one of the deuces for an unmarked ace. One that was unmarked, that is, to the naked eye.

The showdown came. The three cards were slapped face down on the table. Roy studied them, squinting. 'I can't see so good,' he complained. 'Let me borrow your glasses.' And deftly, he appropriated the dealer's 'readers.'

Through the tinted glass, he promptly identified the ace, and pulled in the money.

The mob slunk out of the car, to the jeers of the other passengers. At the next town, a wide place in a muddy road, they jumped the train. Probably they had no funds to ride farther.

As the train pulled out, Roy saw them standing on the deserted platform, shoulders hunched against the cold, naked fear on their pale, gaunt faces. And in the warm comfort of the club car, he shivered for them.

He shivered for himself.

That was where the hit-and-get landed you, where it could land you. This, or something far worse than this, was the fate of the unrooted. Men to whom roots were a hazard rather than an asset. And the big-con boys were no more immune to it than their relatively petty brethren. In fact, their fate was often worse. Suicide. Dope addiction and the d.t.'s. The big house and the nut house.

She sat up, swinging her legs off the bed, and got a cigarette from the reading stand. After it was lit, he took it for himself, and she got herself another.

'Roy,' she said, 'look at me.'

'Oh, I am looking, dear. Believe me, I am.'

'Now, please! Is – is this all we have, Roy? Is it all we're going to have? I'm not knocking it, understand, but shouldn't there be something more?'

'How could we top a thing like that? Tickle each other's feet?'

She looked at him silently, the burning eyes turning lackluster, staring at him from behind an invisible veil.

Without turning her head, she extended a hand and slowly tamped out her cigarette.

'That was a funny,' he said. 'You were supposed to laugh.'

'Oh, I am laughing, dear,' she said. 'Believe me, I am.

She reached down, picked up a stocking and began to draw it on. A little troubled, he pulled her around to face him.

'What are you driving at, Moira? Marriage?'

'I didn't say that.'

'But that's what I asked.'

She frowned, hesitating, then shook her head. 'I don't think so. I'm a very practical little girl, and I don't believe in giving any more than I get. That might be pretty awkward for a matchbook salesman, or whatever you are.'

He was stung, but he kept on playing. 'Would you mind handing me my first aid kit? I think I've just been clawed.'

'Don't worry. Kitty's had all her shots.'

'The fact is, the matchbooks are just a sideline. My real business is running a whorehouse.'

Overhead and income were always in a neck-and-neck race. One sour deal, and they were on the skids.

And it wasn't going to happen to Roy Dillon.

For his first year in Los Angeles, he was strictly a square john. An independent salesman calling on small business-men. Gliding back into the grift, he remained a salesman. And he was still one now. He had a credit rating and a bank account. He was acquainted with literally hundreds of people who would attest to the excellence of his character.

Sometimes they were required to do just that, when suspicion threatened to build into a police matter. But, naturally, he never called upon the same ones twice; and it didn't happen often anyway. Security gave him self-assurance. Security and self-assurance had bred a high degree of skill.

In accomplishing so much, he had had no time for women. Nothing but the casual come-and-go contacts which any young man might have. It was not until late in his third year that he had started looking around for a particular kind of woman. Someone who was not only highly desirable, but who would be willing to – even prefer to – accept the only kind of arrangement which he was willing to offer.

He found her, Moira Langtry, that is, in church.

It was one of those screwball outfits which seem to flourish on the West Coast. The head clown was a yogi or a swami or something of the kind. While his audience listened as though hypnotized, he droned on and on of the Supreme Wisdom of the East, never once explaining why the world's highest incidence of disease, death, and illiteracy endured at the fount of said wisdom.

Roy was a little stunned to find such a one as Moira Langtry present. She just wasn't the type. He was aware of her puzzlement when she saw him, but he had his reasons for being there. It was an innocent way of passing the time. Cheaper than movies and twice as funny. Also, while he was doing very well as it was, he was not blind to the possibility of doing better. And a man just might see a way to do it at gatherings like these.

The audiences were axiomatically boobs. Mostly well-to-do boobs, middle-aged widows and spinsters; women suffering from a vague itch which might be scratched for a bundle. So . . . well, you never knew, did you?

You could keep your eyes open, without going out on a limb.

The clown finished his act. Baskets were passed for the 'Adoration Offering.' Moira tossed her program in one of them, and walked out. Grinning, Dillon followed her.

She was lingering in the lobby, making a business out of pulling on her gloves. As he approached, she looked up with cautious approval.

'Now, what,' he said, 'was a nice girl like you doing in a place like that?'

'Oh, you know.' She laughed lightly. 'I just dropped in for a glass of yogurt.'

'Tsk, tsk. It's a good thing I didn't offer you a martini.'

'It certainly is. I won't settle for less than a double Scotch.'

They took it from there.

It took them rapidly to where they were now. Or reasonable facsimiles thereof.

Lately, today in particular, he sensed that she wanted it to take them somewhat further.

There was just one way of handling that, in his opinion. With the light touch. No one could simultaneously laugh and be serious.

He let his hand walk down her body and come to rest on her navel. 'You know something?' he said. 'If you put a raisin in that, you could pass as a cookie.'

'Don't,' she said, picking up his hand and dropping it to the bed.

'Or you could draw a ring around it, and pretend you're a doughnut.'

'I'm beginning to feel like a doughnut,' she said. 'The part in the middle.'

'Oh, fine. I was afraid it might be something shameful.' Then, cutting him off firmly, pulling him back into line, 'But you see what I'm driving at, Roy. We don't know a thing about each other. We're not friends. We're not even acquainted. It's just been early to bed and early to bed from the time we met.'

'You said you weren't knocking it.'

'I'm not. It's very necessary to me. But I don't feel that it should begin and end with that. It's like trying to live on mustard sandwiches.'

'And you want pâté?'

'Steak. Something nourishing. Aah, hell, Roy' – she shook her head fretfully. 'I don't know. Maybe it isn't on the menu. Maybe I'm in the wrong restaurant.'

'Madame is too cruel! Pierre weel drown heemself in ze soup!'

'Pierre doesn't care,' she said, 'if madame lives or dies. He's made that pretty clear.'

She started to rise, with a certain finality of movement. He caught her and pulled her back to the bed, pulled her body against his again. He felt of her carefully. He smoothed her hair and kissed her lips.

'Mmm, yes,' he said. 'Yes, I'm sure of it. The sale is final, and no exchanges.'

'Here we go again,' she said. 'Out into outer space, before we have our feet on the ground.'

'I mean, I went to a great deal of trouble to find you. A very nice little partridge. Perhaps there are better birds in the bushes, but again there might not be. And – '

' – and a bird in bed is better than a bush. Or something. I'm afraid I'm crabbing your monologue, Roy.'

'Wait!' He held onto her. 'I'm trying to tell you something. That I like you and that I'm lazy. I don't want to look any further. So just show me the price tag, and if I can I'll buy.'

'That's better. I have an idea it might be quite profitable for both of us.'

'So where do we begin? A few evenings on the town? A fling at Las Vegas?'

'Mmm, no, I guess not. Besides, you couldn't afford it.'

'Surprise,' he said curtly. 'I wouldn't even make you pay your own way.'

'Now, Roy . . .' She rumpled his hair affectionately. 'That isn't the kind of thing I have in mind, anyway. A lot of girls, glitter and glassware. If we're going some place, it ought to be at the other end of the street. You know. Relaxed and quiet, so that we can talk for a change.'

'Well. La Jolla's nice this time of year.'

'La Jolla's nice any time of year. But are you sure you can afford – '

'Keep it up,' he warned her. 'One more word of that song, and you'll have the reddest butt in La Jolla. People will think it's another sunset.'

'Pooh! Who's afraid of you?'

'And get the hell out of here, will you? Go crawl back under your culvert! You've drained me dry and got me to splurge my life's savings, and now you want to talk me to death.'

She laughed fondly, and got up. When she was dressed, she knelt again at his bedside for a good-bye kiss.

'Are you sure you're all right, Roy?' She smoothed the hair back from his forehead. 'You look rather pale.'

'Oh, God,' he groaned. 'Will this woman never leave? She puts me through a double shift, and then she says I look pale!'

She left, smiling smugly. Very pleased with herself.

Roy arose wearily, his legs wobbling as he made the round trip to the bathroom. He dropped back down on the bed in a heap, a little worried about himself for the first time. What could be the cause of this, anyway, this strange overpowering fatigue? Not Moira, surely; he was used to her. Not the fact that he had eaten very little during the past three days. He often had spells when he didn't feel hungry, and this had been one of them. Whatever he ate bounced back, in a brownish-colored liquid. Which was strange, since he'd eaten nothing but ice cream and milk.

Frowning, he leaned forward and examined himself. There was a faint purplish-yellow bruise on his stomach. But it didn't hurt any more – unless he pushed on it very hard. He'd had no pain since the day he was slugged.

So . . . ? He shrugged and lay back down. It was just one of those things, he guessed. He didn't feel sick. If a man was sick, he *felt* sick.

He piled the pillows on top of one another, and reclined in a half-sitting position. That seemed to be better, but tired as he was he was restless. With an effort, he reached his trousers from a nearby chair, and dug a quarter from the watch pocket.

Offhand, it looked like any other quarter, but it wasn't quite. The tail side was worn down, the head was not. Holding it back between the fleshy part of his first two fingers, hidden edgewise by them, he could identify the two sides.

He flipped it into the air, caught it and brought it down

against his other hand with a *smack*. For this *was* the smack, one version of it. One of the three standard short-con gimmicks.

'Tails,' he murmured, and there was tails.

He tossed the coin again, and called for heads. And heads came up.

He began closing his eyes on the calls, making sure that he wasn't unconsciously cheating. The coin went up and down, his palm deceptively smacking the back of his hand.

Heads . . . tails . . . heads, heads . . .

And then there was no smack.

His eyes closed, and stayed closed.

That was a little after noon. When he opened them again, twilight was shading the room and the phone was ringing. He looked around wildly, not recognizing where he was, not knowing where he was. Lost in a world that was as strange as it was frightening. Then, drifting back into consciousness, he picked up the phone.

'Yes,' he said; and then, 'What, what? How's that again?' For what the clerk was saying made no sense at all.

'A visitor, Mr Dillon. A very attractive young lady. She says' – a tactful laugh – 'She says she's your mother.'

5

At seventeen going on eighteen, Roy Dillon had left home. He took nothing with him but the clothes he wore – clothes he had bought and paid for himself. He took no money but the little in the pockets of his clothes, and that too he had earned.

He wanted nothing from Lilly. She had given him nothing when he needed it, when he was too small to get for himself, and he wasn't letting her into the game at this late date.

He had no contact with her during the first six months he was away. Then, at Christmas time, he sent her a card, and on Mother's Day he sent her another. Both were of the gooey sentimental type, dripping with sickly sweetness, but the latter was a real dilly. Hearts and flowers and fat little angels swarmed over it in an insanely hilarious montage. The engraved message was dedicated to Dear Old Mom, and it gushed tearfully of goodnight kisses and platters and pitchers of oven-fresh cookies and milk when a little boy came in from play.

You would have thought that Dear Old Mom (God bless her silvering hair) had been the proprietor of a combination dairy-bakery, serving no customer but her own little tyke (on his brand-new bike).

He was laughing so hard when he sent it that he almost botched up the address. But afterward, he had some sobering second thoughts. Perhaps the joke was on him, yes? Perhaps by gibing at her he was revealing a deep and lasting hurt, admitting that she was tougher than he. And that, naturally, wouldn't do. He'd taken everything she had to hand out, and it hadn't made a dent in him. He damned well mustn't ever let her think that it had.

So he kept in touch with her after that, at Christmas and on her birthday and so on. But he was very correct about it. He just didn't think enough of her, he told himself, to indulge in ridicule. It would take a lot better woman than Lilly Dillon to get to him.

The only way he showed his true feelings was in the presents they exchanged. For while Lilly could obviously afford far better gifts than he, he would not admit it. At least, he did not until the effort to keep up with or outdo her not only threatened his long-range objectives, but revealed itself for what it was. Another manifestation of hurt. She had hurt him – or so it looked – and childishly he was rejecting her attempts at atonement.

She might think that, anyway, and he couldn't let her. So he had written her casually that gift-giving had been over-commercialized, and that they should stick to token remembrances from then on. If she wanted to donate to charity in his name, fine. Boys' Town would be appropriate. He, of course, would make a donation in her name.

Say to some institution for Wayward Women . . .

Well, but that is getting ahead of the story, skipping over its principal element.

New York is a two-hour ride from Baltimore. At seventeen going on eighteen, Roy went there, the logical objective of a young man whose only assets were good looks and an inherent yen for the fast dollar.

Needing to earn – and to be paid – immediately, he took work selling on a flat commission. Door-to-door stuff. Magazines, photo coupons, cooking utensils, vacuum cleaners – anything that looked promising. All of it promised much and gave little.

Perhaps Miles of Michigan had made $1,380 his first month by showing Super Suitings to his friends, and perhaps O'Hara of Oklahoma earned ninety dollars a day by taking orders for the Oopsy Doodle Baby Walker. But Roy doubted it like hell. By literally knocking himself out, he made as high as $125 in one week. But that was his very best week. The average was between seventy-five and eighty dollars, and he had to hump to get that.

Still it was better than working as a messenger, or taking some small clerical job which promised 'Good Opportunity' and 'Possibility To Advance' in lieu of an attractive wage. Promises were cheap. Suppose he went to one of those places and promised to be president some day; so how about a little advance?

The selling was no good, but he knew of nothing else. He was very irked with himself. Here he was nineteen going on twenty, and already a proven failure. What was wrong with him, anyway? What had Lilly had that he didn't have?

Then, he stumbled onto the twenties.

It was a fluke. The chump, the proprietor of a cigar store, had really pulled it on himself. Preoccupied, Roy had continued to fumble for a coin after receiving the change from the bill, and the fidgety storekeeper, delayed in waiting on other customers, had suddenly lost patience.

'For Pete's sake, mister!' he snapped. 'It's only a nickel! Just pay me the next time you're in.'

Then, he threw back the twenty, and Roy was a block away before he realized what had happened.

On the heels of the realization came another: an ambitious young man did not wait for such happy accidents. He created them. And he forthwith started to do so.

He was coldly told off at two places. At three others, it was pointed out – more or less politely – that he was not entitled to the return of his twenty. At the remaining three, he collected.

He was exuberant at his good luck. (And he had been exceptionally lucky.) He wondered if there were any gimmicks similar to the twenties, ways of picking up as much money in a few hours as a *fool* made in a week.

There were. He was introduced to them that night in a bar, whence he had gone to celebrate.

A customer sat down next to him, jostling his elbow. A little of his drink was spilled, and the man apologetically insisted on buying him a fresh one. Then he bought still another round. At this point, of course, Roy wanted to buy a round. But the man's attention had been diverted. He was peering down at the floor, then reaching down and picking up a dice cube which he laid on the bar.

'Did you drop this, pal? No? Well, look. I don't like to drink so fast, but if you want to roll me for a round – just to keep things even . . .'

They rolled. Roy won. Which naturally wouldn't do at all. They rolled again, for the price of four drinks, and this time the guy won. And, of course, that wouldn't do either. He just wouldn't allow it. Hell, they were just swapping drinks, friendly like, and he certainly wasn't going to walk out of here winner.

'We'll roll for eight drinks this time. well, call it five bucks even, and then . . .'

The *tat*, with its rapidly doubling bets, is murder on a fool. That is its vicious beauty. Unless he is carrying very heavy, the man *with-the-best-of-it* strips him on a relatively innocent number of winning rolls.

Roy's griftings were down the drain in twenty minutes.

In another ten, all of his honest money had followed it. The guy felt very bad about it; he said so himself. Roy must take back a couple bucks of his loss, and . . .

But the taste of the grift was strong in Roy's mouth, the taste and the smell. He said firmly that he would take back half of the money. The grifter – his name was Mintz – could keep the other half for his services as an instructor in swindling.

'You can begin the lessons right now,' he said. 'Start with that dice gimmick you just worked on me.'

There were some indignant protests from Mintz, some stern language from Roy. But in the end they adjourned to one of the booths, and that night and for some nights afterward they played the roles of teacher and pupil. Mintz held back nothing. On the contrary, he talked almost to the point of becoming tiresome. For here was a blessed chance to drop pretence. He could show how smart he was, as his existence normally precluded doing, and do it in absolute safety.

Mintz did not like the twenties. It took a certain indefinable something which he did not have. And he never worked it without a partner, someone to distract the chump while the play was being made. As for working with a partner, he didn't like that either. It cut the *score* right down the middle. It put an apple on your head, and handed the other guy a shotgun. Because grifters, it seemed, suffered an irresistible urge to beat their colleagues. There was little glory in whipping a fool – hell, fools were made to be whipped. But to take a professional, even if it cost you in the long run, ah, that was something to polish your pride.

Mintz liked the smack. It was natural, you know. Everyone matched coins.

He particularly liked the tat, whose many virtues were almost beyond enumeration. Hook a group of guys on that tat, and you had it made for the week.

The tat must always be played on a very restricted surface, a bar or a booth table. Thus, you could not actually roll the die, although, of course, you appeared to. You shook your hand vigorously, holding the cube on a high point, never shaking it at all, and then you spun it out, letting it skid and topple but never turn. If the marks became suspicious, you shot out of a cup, or, more likely, a glass, since you were in a bar room. But again you did not really shake the die. You held it, as before, clicking it vigorously against the glass in a simulated rattle, and then you spun it out as before.

It took practice, sure. Everything did.

If things got too warm, the bartender would often give you a *take-out* for a good tip. Call you to the phone or say that the cops were coming or something like that. Bartenders were chronically fed up with drinkers. They'd as soon see them chumped as not, if it made them a buck, and unless the guys were their friends.

Mintz knew of many gimmicks other than the three standards. Some of them promised payoffs exceeding the normal short-con top of a thousand dollars. But these invariably required more than one man, as well as considerable time and preparation; were, in short, bordering big-con stuff. And they had one very serious disadvantage: if the fool tipped, you were caught. You hadn't made a mistake. You hadn't just been unlucky. You'd just had it.

There were two highly essential details of grifting which Mintz did not explain to his pupil. One of them defied explanation. It was an acquired trait, something each man had to do on his own and in his own way; i.e., retaining a high degree of anonymity while remaining in circulation. You couldn't disguise yourself, naturally. It was more a matter of *not* doing anything. Of avoiding any mannerism, any expression, any tone or pattern of speech, any posture or gesture or walk – anything at all that might be remembered.

Thus, the first unexplained essential.

Presumably, Mintz didn't explain the second one because he saw no need to. It was something that Roy must certainly know.

The lessons ended.

Roy industriously went to work on the grift. He acquired a handsome wardrobe. He moved to a good hotel. Indulging himself extravagantly, he still built up a roll of more than four thousand dollars.

Months passed. Then, one day, when he was eating in an Astoria-section lunchroom, a detective came in looking for him.

Conferring with the proprietor, he described Roy to a *t*. He had no photo of him, but he did have a police artist's reconstruction, and it was an excellent likeness.

Roy could see them looking down his way, as they talked,

and he thought wildly of running. Of beating it back through the kitchen, and on out the back door. Probably the only thing that kept him from running was the weakness of his legs.

And then he looked at himself in the back-counter mirror, and he breathed a shuddery sigh of relief.

The day had turned warm after he left his hotel, and he'd checked his hat, coat and tie in a subway locker. Then, only an hour or so ago, he'd got a butch-style haircut.

So he was changed, considerably. Enough anyway to keep him from being collared. But he was shaken right down to his shoe soles. He sneaked back to his hotel room, wondering if he'd ever have the guts to work again. He stayed in the hotel until dark, and then he went looking for Mintz.

Mintz was gone from the small hotel where he had lived. He'd left months ago, leaving no forwarding address. Roy started hunting for him. By sheer luck, he found him in a bar six blocks away.

The grifter was horrified when Roy told him what had happened. 'You mean you've been working here all this time? You've been working *steady*? My God! Do you know where I've been in the last six months? A dozen places! All the way to the coast and back!'

'But why? I mean, New York's a big city. Why – '

Mintz cut him off impatiently. New York *wasn't* a big city, he said. It just had a lot of people in it, and they were crammed into a relatively small area. And, no you didn't help your odds much by getting out of jampacked Manhattan and into the other boroughs. Not only did you keep bumping into the same people, people who worked in Manhattan and lived in Astoria, Jackson Heights, et cetera, but you were more conspicuous there. Easier to be spotted by the fools. 'And, kid, a blind man could spot you. Look at that haircut! Look at the fancy wristwatch, and them three-tone sports shoes! Why don't you wear a black eye-patch, too, and a mouthful of gold teeth?'

Roy reddened. He asked troubledly if every city was like this. Did you have to keep jumping from place to place, using up your capital and having to move on just about the time you got to know your way around?

'What do you want?' Mintz shrugged. 'Egg in your beer? You can usually play a fairly long stand in Los Angeles, because it ain't just one town. It's a county full of towns, dozens of 'em. And with traffic so bad and a lousy transportation system, the people don't mix around like they do in New York. *But*' – he wagged a finger severely – 'but that still doesn't mean you can run wild, kid. You're a grifter, see? A thief. You've got no home and no friends, and no visible means of support. And you damned well better not ever forget it.'

'I won't,' Roy promised. 'But, Mintz . . .'

'Yeah?'

Roy smiled and shook his head, keeping his thought to himself. *Suppose I did have a home, a regular place of residence? Suppose I had hundreds of friends and acquaintances? Suppose I had a job and –*

And there was a knock on the door, and he said, 'Come in, Lilly,' and his mother came in.

6

She didn't seem to have aged a year in the seven since he'd last seen her. He was twenty-five, now, which meant that she was crowding thirty-nine. But she appeared to be in her very early thirties, say about thirty-one or -two. She looked like . . . like . . . Why, of course! Moira Langtry! That was who she reminded him of. You couldn't say that they actually *looked* like each other; they were both brunettes and about the same size, but there was absolutely no facial resemblance. It was more a type similarity than a personal one. They were both members of the same flock; women who knew just what it took to preserve and enhance their natural attractiveness. Women who were either endowed with what it took, or spared no effort in getting it.

Lilly took a chair diffidently, unsure of her welcome, quickly explaining that she was in Los Angeles on business. 'I'm handling playback money at the tracks, Roy. I'll be getting back to Baltimore as soon as the races are over.'

Roy nodded equably. The explanation was reasonable. Playback – knocking the odds down on a horse by heavy pari-mutuel betting – was common in big-time bookmaking.

'I'm glad to see you, Lilly. I'd have been hurt if you hadn't dropped by.'

'And I'm glad to see you, Roy. I – ' She looked around the room, leaning forward a little to peer into the bathroom. Slowly, her diffidence gave way to a puzzled frown. 'Roy,' she said. 'What's this all about? Why are you living in a place like this?'

'What's wrong with it?'

'Stop kidding me! It isn't you, that's what wrong. Just look at it! Look at those corny clown pictures! That's a sample of my son's taste? Roy Dillon goes for corn?'

Roy would have laughed if he hadn't been so weak. The four pictures were his own additions to the decorations. Concealed in their box frames was his grifted dough. Fifty-two thousand dollars in cash.

He murmured that he had rented the place as he found it, the best that he could afford. After all, he was just a commission salesman and . . .

'And that's another thing,' Lilly said. 'Four years in a town like Los Angeles, and a peanut selling job is the best you can do! You expect me to believe that? It's a front, isn't it? This dump is a front. You're working an angle, and don't tell me you're not because I wrote the book!'

'Lilly . . .' His faint voice seemed to come from miles away. 'Lilly, mind your own damned business . . .'

She said nothing for a moment, recovering from his rebuke, reminding herself that he was more stranger than son. Then, half-pleading, 'You don't have to do it, Roy. You've got so much on the ball – so much more than I ever had – and . . . You know what it does to a person, Roy. I – '

His eyes were closed. An apparent signal to shut up or get out. Forcing a smile, she said, Okay, she wouldn't start scolding the minute she saw him.

'Why are you still in bed – s-son? Are you sick?'

'Nothing,' he muttered. 'Just . . .'

She came over to the side of the bed. Timidly, she put the palm of her hand to his forehead; let out a startled gasp. 'Why, Roy, you're ice cold! What – ' Light bloomed over his pillows as she switched on the table lamp. He heard another gasp. 'Roy, what's the matter? You're as white as a sheet!'

'Nothin' . . .' His lips barely moved. 'No s-sweat, Lilly.'

Suddenly, he had become terribly frightened. He knew, without knowing why, that he was dying. And with the terrible fear of death was an unbearable sadness. Unbearable because there was no one who cared, no one to assuage it. No one, no one at all, to share it with him.

Only one death, Roy? Well, what are you kicking about?

But they can't eat you, can they? They can kill you, but they can't eat you.

'Don't!' he sobbed, his voice pushing up through an overpowering drowsiness. 'D-don't laugh at me – I – '

'I won't! I'm not laughing, honey! I – Listen to me, Roy!' She squeezed his hand fiercely. 'You don't seem to be sick. No fever or – Where do you hurt? Did someone hurt you?'

He didn't hurt. There had been no pain since the day of his slugging. But . . .

'Hit . . .' he mumbled. 'Three days ago . . .'

'Three days ago? How? Where were you hit? What – Wait a minute, darling! Just wait until mother makes a phone call, and then – '

In what was record time for the Grosvenor-Carlton, she got an outside line. She spoke over the phone, her voice cracking like a whip.

'. . . Lilly Dillon, doctor. I work for Justus Amusement

Company out of Baltimore, and – *What?* Don't you brush me off, buster! Don't tell me you never heard of me! If I have to have Bobo Justus call you – ! Well, all right then. Let's see how fast you can get over here!'

She slammed down the receiver, and turned back to Roy.

The doctor came, out of breath and looking a little sullen; then, forgetting his wounded dignity, as his eyes drank in Lilly.

'So sorry if I was abrupt, Mrs Dillon. Now, don't tell me this strapping young man can be your son!'

'Never mind that.' Lilly chopped off his flattery. 'Do something for him. I think he's in a pretty bad way.'

'Well, now. Let's just see.'

He moved past her, looked down at the pale figure on the bed. Abruptly, his light manner washed away, and his hand moved quickly; testing Roy's heart, probing for pulse and blood pressure.

'How long has he been like this, Mrs Dillon?' – curtly, not turning to look at her.

'I don't know. He was in bed when I came in about an hour ago. We talked and he seemed to be all right, except that he kept getting weaker and – '

'I'll bet he did! Any history of ulcers?'

'No. I mean, I'm not sure. I haven't seen him in seven years, and – What's the matter with him, doctor?'

'Do you know whether he's been in any kind of accident during the last few days? Anything that might have injured him internally?'

'No . . .' She corrected herself again. 'Well, yes, he was! He was trying to tell me about it. Three days ago, he was hit in the stomach – some barroom drunk, I suppose . . .'

'Any vomiting afterward? Coffee-colored?' The doctor

yanked down the sheet, nodding grimly at sight of the bruise. 'Well?'

'I don't know . . .'

'What's his blood-type? Do you know that?'

'No. I – '

He dropped the sheet, and picked up the phone. As he summoned an ambulance, breaking the hotel's outside call record for the second time that day, he stared at Lilly with a kind of worried reproach.

He hung up the phone. 'I wish you'd known his blood type,' he said. 'If I could have got some blood into him now, instead of having to wait until he's typed . . .'

'Is it . . . He'll be all right, won't he?'

'We'll do all we can. Oxygen will help some.'

'But will he be all right?'

'His blood-pressure is under a hundred, Mrs Dillon. He's had an internal hemorrhage.'

'Stop it!' She wanted to scream at him. 'I asked you a question! I asked you if – '

'I'm sorry,' he said evenly. 'The answer is no. I don't think he can live until he gets to the hospital.'

Lilly swayed. She got hold of herself; drawing herself straight, making her voice firm. And she spoke to the doctor very quietly.

'My son will be all right,' she said. 'If he isn't, I'll have you killed.'

7

Carol Roberg arrived at the hospital at five in the afternoon, an hour before the beginning of her shift. The mere thought of being late to work terrified her, and, by coming so early, she could get a bargain-priced meal in the employee's cafeteria before going on duty. That was very important to Carol – a good meal at a low price. Even when she wasn't hungry, which was seldom, even in America where no one seemed ever to be hungry, she was always subtly worried about when she would eat again.

Her white nurse's uniform was so stiffly starched that it gave off little pops and crackles as she hurried down the marble corridor. Cut overlong, in the European fashion, it made her look like a child dressed in its mother's clothes; and the skirt and cuffs flared upward at the corners, seeming to set a pattern for her eyes, her mouth, her brows, and the tips of her short bobbed hair. All her features had an amusing turned-up look, and no amount of inner solemnity could conquer it. In fact, the more solemn she was, the more determinedly severe, the greater was the effect of suppressed laughter: a child playing at being a woman.

Entering the cafeteria, she moved straight to the long

serving counter. Blushing self-consciously; careful to avoid looking at anyone who might be looking her way. Several times, here and elsewhere, she had been drawn into joining other diners. And the experience had been painfully awkward. The men, interns and technicians, made jokes which were beyond her limited idiom, so that she never knew quite what her response should be. As for the other nurses, they were nice enough; they wanted to be friendly. But there was a great gulf between them which only time could bridge. She did not talk or think or act as they did, and they seemed to take her ways as a criticism of theirs.

Carol took a tray and silverware from the serving counter, and studied the steamy expanse of food. Carefully, weighing each item against the other, she made her selections.

Potatoes and gravy were eight cents. Then the two-order would be fifteen, yes? A penny less.

'The two-order – ?' The fat counter woman laughed. 'Oh, you mean a double?'

'A double, yes. It is fifteen?'

The woman hesitated, looked around conspiratorially. 'Tell you what, honey. We'll make it the same price as a single, hmm? I'll just go a little bit heavy with the spoon.'

'You can do this?' Carol's turned-up eyes rounded with awe. 'It would not cause trouble?'

'For me? Hah! I *own* this joint, honey.'

Carol guessed that that made it all right. It would not be stealing. Her conscience comfortable, she also accepted the two extra sausages which the woman buried beneath her order of knockwurst and sauerkraut.

She was hesitating at the dessert section, about to decide that she could have a strudel in view of her other economies, when she heard the voices back down the line: the fat woman talking to another attendant.

'. . . *Kosher Kid can really put it away, can't she?*'

'*When she gets it for nothin', sure. That's how them kikes get ahead.*'

Carol froze for a moment. Then, stiffly, she moved on, paying her check and carrying her tray to a table in a distant corner of the room. She began to eat, methodically; forcing down the suddenly tasteless food until it once again became tasteful and desirable.

That was the way one had to do. To do the best one could, and accept things as they were. Usually, they did not seem so bad after a while; if they were not actually good, then they became so by virtue of the many things that were worse. Almost everything was relatively good. Eating was better than starving, living better than dying.

Even a simulated friendliness was better than none at all. People had to care – at least a little – to pretend. Her own kith and kind, immigrants like herself, had not always done that.

She had come to the United States under the auspices of relatives, an aunt and uncle who had fled Austria before the *anschluss*. Now well-to-do, they had taken her into their home and given her probationary status as a daughter. But with certain unstated stipulations: that she become one with them, that she live as they lived, without regard to how she had lived before. And Carol could not do that.

The ritual dining, the numerous sets of dishes, each to be used only for a certain kind of food, were almost offensive to her. So much waste in a world filled with want! Contrariwise, it seemed foolish to fast in the midst of abundance.

She was repelled by the bearded, pink-mouthed *Shiddem*

for all his Judaic learning. To her he seemed a parasite, who should be forced to work as others did. She was shocked to find stupidity masquerading as pride – or what she thought of as stupidity: the imperviousness to a new language, and a new and possibly better way of life. All in all she was frightened by the conscientious apartness, sensing in it the seeds of tragedy.

Because they were good to her, or meant to be, she tried to be as they were. She was even willing to believe that they were right and that she was wrong. But mere trying, willingness, was not enough for them. They accused her of abandoning her faith, one that she could never remember knowing. Their tyranny, in its own way, seemed almost as bad as that she had fled from, and at last, she had had to flee from them.

Life outside the refugee world wasn't easy. The alternative to it often seemed to be a world with quite as many prejudices as the one she had left. But it was not always that way. There were some people who were completely indifferent to what she had been; that is, they were indifferent in a critical sense. They – the rare few: Mrs Dillon was their best example – accepted her for what she was *now*. And –

She saw Mrs Dillon approaching, moving past the other tables with her easy imperiousness. Hastily, Carol set down her teacup and came to her feet.

'Please sit down, Mrs Dillon. I will get you some tea, yes? Some coffee? Something to eat – '

'Nothing,' Lilly smiled, waving her back to her chair. 'I won't be staying at the hospital this evening, and I wanted to talk to you before I left.'

'There is something wrong? I – I have done – '

'No, you're doing just fine. Everything's fine,' Lilly

assured her. 'Get yourself some more tea, if you like. There's no hurry.'

'I'd better not.' Carol shook her head. 'It is almost six, and the other nurse – '

'I'm paying the other nurse, too,' Lilly said flatly. 'She's working for me, not the hospital. If she doesn't want to work a little overtime for extra pay, she can quit.'

Carol nodded and murmured meekly. This was a side of Mrs Dillon she had never seen before. Lilly's smile returned.

'Now, just relax and rest easy, Carol. I like your work. I like you. I hope you like me, too – my son and I.'

'Oh, I do, very much! You have been very nice to me.'

'Why is it that you don't have a regular job? That you're just working extra?'

'Well . . .' Carol hesitated over her answer. 'The hospital, almost every hospital, it graduates its own nurses, and I am not such a graduate. Then, the regular jobs, like in the doctors' offices, they usually want skills that I do not have. Often bookkeeping and shorthand, and – '

'I understand. How do you make out on this special duty work? All right?'

'Well, I do not always make so much,' Carol said seriously. 'It depends on how much work I can get, and that is not always a great deal. And, of course, there are the fees to the nurses' registry. But . . . well, it is enough, whatever. When I know more and when I better understand English – '

'Yeah, sure. How old are you, Carol?'

'Twenty-seven.'

'Oh?' Lilly was surprised. 'I wouldn't have thought you were that old.'

'I feel much older, sometimes. Like I had lived forever. But, yes, I am twenty-seven.'

'Well, no matter. Any boy friends? Going steady with anyone? No?' Lilly thought that was strange too. 'Now, a girl like you must have had plenty of opportunities.'

Carol shook her head, her upturned features humorously solemn. She lived in a furnished room, she pointed out, and she could not properly receive young men in it. Then, since it was necessary to work whenever she could, and since she worked irregular hours, it was not possible to plan ahead nor to be sure of keeping a social engagement if any were made.

'Also,' she concluded, blushing, 'also, the young men try to do certain things. They – often, I am greatly embarrassed.'

Lilly nodded gently, feeling a strange tenderness toward the girl. Here was something, someone, absolutely real and the reality was all to the good. Perhaps, under different circumstances, she might have turned out as wholesome and honest – and *real* – as Carol was. But – she shook herself mentally – to hell with that noise.

She was what she was, and thus Roy had become what he was. And there was nothing to be done about her, assuming that she wanted anything done, but perhaps it wasn't too late to . . .

'You're probably wondering why I was so nosy. Inquisitive, I mean,' Lilly said. 'Well, it's like this. I don't want to jinx my son by saying that he's going to be all right, but – '

'Oh, I'm sure he will be, Mrs Dillon! I – '

'Don't say it,' Lilly said sharply, knocking on the wooden top of the table. 'It might bring bad luck. Let's just say that when and if he is able to leave the hospital, I'd like you to go on looking after him for a while. At my apartment, I mean. Do you think you'd like that?'

Carol nodded eagerly, her eyes shining. She'd already had more than two weeks of steady employment with Mrs Dillon, more than she'd ever had before. What a wonderful thing it would be to go on working for her and her nice son, indefinitely.

'Well, that's fine, then,' Lilly said. 'It's all settled. Now, I've got to run along, but – Yes?'

'I was just wondering . . .' Carol hesitated. 'I was wondering if – if Mr Dillon would want me. He is always very kind, but . . .' She hesitated again, not knowing how to say what she meant without sounding impolite. Lilly said it for her.

'You mean Roy resents me. He's against anything I do simply because I do it.'

'Oh, no. I did not mean that. Not exactly, anyway. I was just . . .'

'Well, it's close enough,' Lilly smiled, trying to make her voice light. 'But don't worry about it, dear. You're working for me not him. Anything I do for him is for his own good, so it doesn't matter if he's a little resentful at first.'

Carol nodded, a trifle dubiously. Lilly arose from her chair, and began drawing on her gloves.

'We'll just keep this to ourselves for the time being,' she said. 'It's just possible that Roy will suggest it himself.'

'Whatever you say,' Carol murmured.

They walked to the door of the cafeteria together. Then Lilly headed toward the lobby entrance, and Carol hurried away toward her patient's room.

The other nurse left as soon as they had checked the

chart together. Roy gave Carol a weakly lazy grin, and told her she looked very bad.

'You belong in bed, Miss Roberg,' he said. 'I'll give you part of mine.'

'I do *not!*' Carol blushed furiously. 'You will *not!*'

'Oh, but you do. I've seen girls with that look before. Bed is the only thing that will cure 'em.'

Carol giggled unwillingly, feeling very wicked. Roy told her severely that she mustn't laugh about such things. 'You'd better behave or I won't kiss you goodnight. Then, you'll be sorry!'

'I will *not!*' Carol blushed and wriggled and giggled. 'Now, you stop *it!*'

Roy stopped the teasing after a minute or two. She was honestly embarrassed by it, he guessed, and he wasn't up to much fun-making himself.

Suspended from a metal stand on the left side of his bed was a jar of syrupy-looking blood. A tube extended from the upended top of it to a quill-like needle in his arm. On the right side of the bed, a similar device dripped saline water into the artery of his other arm. The blood and water had been fed into him thus since his arrival in the hospital. Lying constantly on his back with his arms held flat, he ached almost incessantly, his only relief coming when his body and arms became numb. Sometimes he found himself wondering if life was worth such a price. But the wondering was humorous, strictly on the wry side.

He'd had a long look at death, and he hadn't liked the look of it at all.

He was very, very glad to be alive.

Now that he was apparently out of danger, however, he did regret one thing – that it was Lilly who had saved his life. The one person to whom he wished to owe nothing, he now owed everything, a debt he could never repay.

He could fret and argue the matter in his mind. He could cite his own incredibly tough constitution, an irresible will to live, as the true source of his survival. The doctors themselves had practically said as much, hadn't they? It was scientifically impossible, they'd said, for a man to live when his blood pressure and hemoglobin fell below a certain level. Yet his had been well below that level *when* he arrived at the hospital. Unassisted, he had been clinging to life on his own *before* anything had been done for him. So . . .

So nothing. He'd needed help fast, and Lilly had got it for him. Moira hadn't seen his need, he hadn't, no one had but Lilly. And just where, for that matter, had he got the mental and physical toughness to hold on until he had medical help? From strangers? Huh-uh.

Any way you looked at it, he owed his life to Lilly. And Lilly, unconsciously or deliberately, was making sure that he didn't forget it.

In a sweetly feline fashion, she'd put such a frost on Moira Langtry that Moira had stopped coming to the hospital after a couple of visits. She called every day, letting him know that she was concerned about him, but she didn't come back again. And Lilly often managed to be on hand at the time of her calls, practically restricting his end of the conversation to monosyllables.

Lilly obviously intended to break up his affair with Moira. Nor did her intentions end there. She'd selected a day nurse for him who was a real turtle, competent enough but homely as a mud fence. Then, by contrast, she'd picked a little doll for night duty, a kid that was bound to appeal to him even if Lilly hadn't given her a clear field with no competition.

Oh, he could see what was happening. Everywhere he looked, he could see the shadow of Lilly's fine hand. And just what could he do about it, anyway? Tell her to get the hell away and leave him alone? Could he say, 'Okay, you saved my life; does that give you any claim on me?'

A doctor came in, not the one who had visited at the hotel – Lilly had dismissed him right at the beginning – but a merry-looking young man. Behind him came an orderly, wheeling a metal-topped cart. Roy looked at the implements on it, and let out a groan.

'Oh, no! Not that thing again!'

'You mean you don't like it?' The doctor laughed. 'He's kidding us, isn't he, nurse? He loves to have his stomach pumped.'

'Please.' Carol frowned reprovingly. 'It is not funny.'

'Aah, you can't hurt this guy. Rally round now, and we'll get it over with.'

The orderly held him on one side, one hand clamping over the intravenous needle. Carol held the needle into the other arm, her free hand poised over a bowl of tiny ice cubes. The doctor picked up a narrow rubber tube and pushed it up into his nose.

'Now, hold still, keedo. Hold still or you'll jerk those needles loose!'

Roy tried to hold still but he couldn't. As the tube went up into his nose and down into his throat, he jerked and struggled. Gagging, gasping for breath, he tried to break free of them. And the doctor cursed him merrily, and Carol pressed little ice lumps between his lips.

'Please to swallow, Mr Dillon. Swallow the ice and the tube will go down with it.'

Roy kept swallowing. At last the tube was down his throat and into his stomach. The doctor made some minor adjustments in it, moving it up and down slightly.

'How's that? Not hitting bottom, is it?'

Roy said he didn't think so. It seemed to be all right.

'Good.' The doctor checked the glass receptacle to which the pump was attached. 'I'll be back in thirty minutes, nurse. If he gives you any trouble, sock him in the stomach.'

Carol nodded coldly. She looked after him, frowning, as he strode out of the room, then came over to the bed and patted away the sweat from Roy's face.

'I am sorry. I hope it does not bother you too much.'

'It's all right.' He felt a little abashed at the fuss he had made. 'I'm just kind of conscious of it, you know.'

'I know. The worst part is getting it down, but afterward it is not good. You cannot swallow well and your breathing is ever-so-slightly hampered, and never do you become accustomed to it. Always, there is the consciousness of something wrong.'

'You sound like you'd been pumped yourself.'

'I have been, many times.'

'Internal bleeding?'

'No. I began to bleed after a time, but I was not bleeding to begin with.'

'Yes?' he frowned. 'I don't get you. Why were you being pumped out if – '

'I don't know.' She smiled suddenly and shook her head. 'It was a very long time ago. Anyway, it is not pleasant to talk about.'

'But – '

'And I think you should not talk so much, either. You will just lie still, please, and do nothing to disturb your stomach contents.'

'I don't see how there could be any contents.'

'Well, anyway,' she said firmly. And he let it go at that.

It was easy to drop the subject. Easy, in his insistent need to survive, to ignore all possible distractions. Years of practice had made it so easy that it was almost automatic.

He lay quietly, watching Carol as she moved about the room, seeing her youthful freshness as a refreshing relief from Moira. A very nice little kid, he thought, just about as nice as they came. So doubtless she must be left that way. On the other hand, wouldn't it be a little strange if a girl as attractive as she was had remained strictly on the nice side? Weren't the odds all against it? And if she did know the score . . .

Well, it was something to think about. Certainly, it would be a pleasant way of putting Lilly in her place.

The doctor returned. He checked the glass container of the pump, and chortled happily. 'Nothing but bile. That's what he's full of, nurse, as if you didn't know.'

He removed the stomach tube. Then, wonder of wonders, he ordered the intravenous needles removed from Roy's arms. 'Why not? Why should we baby a goldbrick like you?'

'Oh, go to hell.' Roy grinned at him, flexing his arms luxuriously. 'Just let me stretch.'

'Sassy, hmm. How about something to eat?'

'You mean that liquid chalk you call milk? Bring it on, brother.'

'Nope. Tonight you get steak, mashed potatoes, the works. You can even have a couple of cigarettes.'

'You're kidding.'

The doctor shook his head, became serious. 'You haven't bled any in three days. It's time your stomach resumed peristalsis, started toughening itself up, and it can't do it on liquids.'

Roy was just a little uneasy. After all, it was his stomach. The doctor assured him that he had nothing to worry about.

'If your stomach won't take it, we'll just have to open you up and cut out a piece. No trouble at all.'

He walked out, whistling.

Again, Carol looked after him, frowning. 'That man! Ooh, I would like to shake him good!'

'You think it will be all right?' Roy asked. 'To have solid food. I mean. I'm not particularly hungry, and – '

'Of course, it will be all right! Otherwise, you would not be allowed to have it.'

She took one of his hands in hers, looked down at him so protectively that he wanted to smile. He restrained the impulse, clinging to her hand while he gently urged her into the chair at his side.

'You're a good little girl,' he said softly. 'I've never known anyone like you.'

'T-thank you . . .' Her eyes fell, and her voice dropped to a whisper. 'I have known no one like you either.'

He lay studying her in the gathering twilight of the room, examining the small honest face with its tenderly upturning features; thinking how much she looked like some gravely innocent child. Then he turned on his side, and eased over near the edge of the bed.

'I'm going to miss you, Carol. Will I see you after I leave here?'

'I – I do not know.' She was breathing heavily, still not

looking at him. 'I – I would like to, b-but I must work whenever I can, whenever I am c-called and – '

'Carol?'

'Y-yes?'

'Come here.'

He drew her forward by the hand, his free hand dropping around her shoulders. She looked up at last, eyes frightened, hanging back desperately. And then, suddenly, she was in his arms, her face pressed against his.

'Like me, Carol?'

'Oh, yes!' her head jerked in assent. 'So, so much! B-but – '

'Listen,' he said. And then as she listened, waiting, he was silent. Putting on the brakes. Telling himself that this was as far as it should go.

But was it? He would need looking after for a while, wouldn't he? Lilly had hinted at something of the kind, suggesting that he stay in her apartment for a week or so. He'd been against it, of course, first because it was her suggestion, and secondly because it seemed pointless. With her away at the tracks so much, he'd still be on his own. But . . .

Carol shivered against him delicately. He started to shove her away; and, unwillingly, his arms tightened around her.

'I was just thinking,' he said. 'I'll still be a little rocky after I leave here. Maybe – '

'Yes?' She raised her head, smiled down at him excitedly. 'You would want me to tend you for a while, yes? That is it?'

'You'd like that?'

'Yes! Oh, my, yes!'

'Well,' he said, awkwardly. 'We'll think about it. See what my mother has to say. I live in a hotel myself, so I'd have to stay at her place. And – '

'And it will be all right!' Her eyes were dancing. 'I know.'

'How do you mean?'

'I mean, it is what your mother wants! I – we were not going to say anything about it yet. She was not sure how you would feel, and – and – '

Her voice died away under his flat-eyed stare. Quick anxiety tugged at the tipped-up corners of her mouth.

'Please. T-there is something wrong?'

'Not a thing,' he said. 'No, sir, everything's just fine.

8

The fourth race was over. The backside crowds surged back through the areaway which passed beneath the grandstand, and led into the vaulted arena of bars, lunchrooms, and pari-mutuel windows. Some of them were hurrying, smiling broadly, or wearing smug, tight-lipped grins. They headed toward pay-off windows. Others, the majority, came more slowly, scanning their racing programs, tip sheets, and forms; their faces indifferent, desperate, angry, or sullen. These were the losers, and some of them went on through the exits to the parking lot, and some stopped at the bars, and most of them moved toward the bet windows.

It was still early in the day. There were still a lot of full pockets. The crowd would not shake out much before the end of the sixth race.

Lilly Dillon collected three bets at as many windows. Putting the money to one side in her purse – for it would have to be accounted for – she hurried toward the bet windows. Her betting money, the playback dough that came by wire each day, was already separated into sheafs of twenties, fifties, and hundreds. She used the twenties as much as her limited time would allow, usually five and ten at a time. With the fifties she was more cautious; the hundreds were disposed of with downright stinginess.

Possibly, rather probably, much of her caution was wasted. The treasury agents had no interest in the betting; they were normally on the lookout only for wins, the cashing in of fistfuls of fifty and hundred-dollar tickets. And Lilly was not there to win, and seldom did. Her activities were largely precautionary, not usually concerned with favorites or semi-favorites. The odds on such horses pretty much took care of themselves. She dealt mainly in 'likely' runners and long-shots, and they rarely wound up in the money. When they did, she collected on them only when it seemed absolutely safe. If it didn't, she simply let the winnings go, keeping the pari-mutuel tickets as a matter of record.

To an extent, she was a free agent. She had certain general instructions, but within them she was allowed and expected to use her own judgment. That didn't make things any easier for her, of course. On the contrary. It was a hard job, and she was well paid for it. And there were ways of adding to that pay.

Ways which Bobo Justus frowned upon, but which were very difficult to detect.

She strolled off toward one of the bars, her eyes shrewdly watchful behind the dark sunglasses. Several times she stooped quickly and picked up a discarded ticket, adding them to the ones in her purse. Losing tickets were usually thrown away. As long as they weren't torn or suspiciously trampled, she could count them as money spent.

A certain number of them, anyway. It wasn't something you could lean on too hard. She'd only gone overboard once at this meet, and that had been a mistake. Rather, she'd done it to cover a mistake.

It had happened almost three weeks ago, right after Roy had gone into the hospital. Perhaps that was how it had come about, she'd had her mind on him instead of her job. But, anyway, a real dog had come in at a hundred-and-forty for two. And she didn't have a dime down on him.

She'd been too frightened and worried to sleep that night. She'd been even more frightened the next day when the papers hinted at heavy off-track betting on the nag. As an expensive but necessary precaution, she'd sent five thousand dollars of her own money back to Baltimore – her pretended winnings on the horse. And apparently that had taken the heat off of her, for she'd had no word from Bobo. But days passed before she was resting easy.

For a while, she was even carrying a gun when she went to the bathroom.

She stood at the bar, sipping a rum and cola, looking at the milling crowd with something approaching disgust. Where did they come from? she thought wearily. Why did they buck a stupid racket like this? Many of them were downright shabby. Some of them even had children with them.

Mothers with kids ... Men in cheap sport-shirts and baggy slacks ... Grandmothers with cigarettes dangling from their mouths.

Gaah! It was enough to turn a person's stomach.

She turned away from them, shifting wearily from foot to foot. She was wearing a sports outfit; a simple but expensive ensemble of fawn-colored slacks, blouse, and jacket, with flat-heeled buckskin oxfords. Everything was cool and lightweight, the most comfortable things she could put on. But nothing could compensate for her hours of standing.

As the fifth and sixth races dragged by, as she moved back and forth from the betting and pay-off windows, the struggle between her growing tiredness and the never-ending need to be alert almost reached a stalemate. It was hard to think of anything but sitting down, of resting for at least a few minutes. It was impossible to think about it. Need and necessity fought with one another, pulling her this way and that, tugging her forward and holding her back; adding unbearably to the burden she already carried.

There were seats in the grandstand, of course, but those were for yokels. By the time she got into the stands, she would be due at the windows. The effort of going back and forth would take more from her than it gave. As for the clubhouse, with its comfortable chairs and pleasant cocktail lounge, well, naturally, that was out. There was too much money floating around, too much heavy betting. The treasury boys loved the place.

She set down her cup of coffee – her third in the last hour – and trudged away toward the mutuel windows. The seventh race, the next to the last, was coming up. It always drew some of the day's heaviest play, and the yokels were rushing to buy tickets. As Lilly pushed her way through them, a sardonic thought suddenly struck her. And despite her weariness, she almost laughed out loud.

Now, isn't this something? she thought. Twenty-five years getting out of the mob, and I'm right back in it. Hell, I've never even been away!

She collected a couple of bets on the seventh, disposing of the money as she hurried toward the parking lot. There was nothing in the last race that couldn't be missed. By beating it out now, before the crowd swarmed down from the stands, she could avoid the last-minute traffic jam.

Her car was parked back near the gate, in a space as near to it as a big tip would buy. A convertible, it was a very good car but by no means the most expensive. Not even faintly flashy. Its one distinctive feature was something that couldn't be seen. A secret trunk compartment containing one hundred and thirty thousand dollars in cash.

As she approached the car now and saw the man standing beside it, Lilly wondered whether she'd ever live to spend the money.

9

Bobo Justus had wavy, iron-gray hair and a deeply tanned, chiseled-looking face. He was a small man, short that is, but he had the head and torso of a six-footer. Knowing his sensitivity about his height, Lilly was grateful for her flat-heeled shoes. That was one thing in her favor at least. But she doubted that it would count for much, judging by his expression.

He addressed her tonelessly, his lips barely moving.

'You goddamned silly-looking pig! Driving a goddamned circus wagon! Why don't you paint a bull's-eye on it? Hang a couple of cowbells on the bumper?'

'Now, Bo. Convertibles are quite common in California.'

'Convertibles are quite common in California,' he mimicked her, weaving his shoulders prissily. 'Are they as common as two-timing, double-crossing whores? Hah? Are they, you sneaky little slut?'

'Bo' – she looked around quickly. 'Hadn't we better go some place private?'

He drew back a hand as though to slap her, then gave her a shove toward the car. 'Get with it,' he said. 'The Beverly Hills. I get you alone, and I'm going to pop every pimple on your pretty pink butt!'

She started the car and drove out through the gate. As they joined the stream of town-bound traffic, he resumed his tight-lipped abuse.

Lilly listened attentively, trying to decide whether he was building up steam or letting it off. Probably the last, she guessed, since it had been almost three weeks since her blunder. Murderously angry, he probably would have taken action before this.

Most of the time she was silent, making no response except when it was asked for or seemed urgently indicated.

'. . . told you to watch that fifth race, didn't I? And, by God, you really watched it, didn't you? I bet you stood there grinning clear to your ankles while the dog comes in at a hundred-and-forty per!'

'Bo, I – '

'How much did your pals cut you in for, huh? Or did they give you the same kind of screwing you gave me? What the hell are you, anyway – a stud-horse with tits?'

'I was down on the nag,' Lilly said quietly. 'You know I was, Bo. After all, you wouldn't have wanted me to bet it off the board.'

'You were down on it, huh? Now, I'll ask you just one question. Do you want to stick to that story, or do you want to keep your teeth?'

'I want to keep my teeth.'

'Now, I'll ask you one more question. Do you think I got no contacts out here? You think I couldn't get a report on the play on that horse?'

'No, I don't think that. I'm sure you could, Bo.'

'That nag paid off at just the opening price. There wasn't hardly a flutter on the tote board from the time the odds were posted.' He lit a cigarette, took a couple of quick angry puffs. 'What kind of crap you handing me anyway, Lilly? There ain't enough action to tickle the tote, but you claim a five-grand win! Now, how about it, huh? You ready to fly straight or not?'

She drew in a deep breath. Hesitated. Nodded. There was only one thing to do now, to tell the truth and hope for the best.

She did so. Justus sat turned in the seat; studying, analyzing her expression throughout the recital. When she had finished, he faced back around again, sat in deadpan silence for several minutes.

'So you were just stupid,' he said. 'Asleep at the switch. You think I'm going to buy that?'

Lilly nodded evenly. He'd already bought it, she said, three weeks ago; suspected the truth before he was told. 'You know you did, Bo. If you hadn't, I'd be dead by now.'

'Maybe you will be yet, sister! Maybe you'll wish you was dead.'

'Maybe.'

'I laid out better than a hundred yards for a screwing. Just about the highest-priced piece of tail in history. I figure on getting what I paid for.'

'Then you'd better do some more figuring,' Lilly said. 'I'm not that kind of punching bag.'

'Real sure about that, are you?'

'Positive. Give me a cigarette, please.'

He took a cigarette from his package, and tossed it across the seat. She picked it up, and tossed it back to him.

'Light it please, Bo? I need both hands in this traffic.'

She heard a sound, something between a laugh and a snort, anger and admiration. Then, he lit the cigarette and placed it between her lips.

As they rode on, she could sense the looks he slanted at her, almost see the workings of his mind. She was a problem to him. A very special and valued employee, one whom he actually liked, had yet erred badly. It was unintentional, her one serious mistake in more than twenty years of faithful service. So there was strong argument for forgiveness. On the other hand, he was showing unusual forbearance in allowing her to live, and more hardly seemed to be indicated.

Obviously, there was much to be said for both sides of the debate. Having forgiven so much, he could forgive completely. Or having forgiven so much, he need forgive no more.

They were almost at the hotel before he reached his decision.

'I got a lot of people working for me, Lilly. I can't have things like this happening.'

'It never happened before, Bo.' She fought to keep her voice level, free of any hint of begging. 'It won't happen again.'

'It happened once,' he said. 'With me, that's practically making a habit of it.'

'All right,' she said. 'You're calling the shots.'

'You got any kind of long coat in the car? Anything you can wear home over your clothes?'

'No.' A dull ache came into her stomach.

He hesitated, then said it didn't matter. He'd lend her his raincoat. 'Ought to be right in style out here. Goddamnedest sloppiest-looking women I ever seen.'

She stopped the car at the hotel entrance, and an attendant took charge of it. Bobo handed her out to the steps, then courteously gave her his arm as they entered the building. They crossed the lobby, Bobo holding himself very erect, and entered the elevator.

He had a suite on the fourth floor. Unlocking the door, he motioned for her to precede him. She did so, letting her body go limp, preparing herself for what she knew was coming. But you could never prepare for a thing like that – not fully. The sudden shove-blow sent her hurtling into the room, stumbling and tripping over her own feet. And finally landing in a skidding sprawl on the floor.

As she slowly picked herself up, he locked the door, drew the shades, and entered the bathroom, emerging immediately with a large towel. Crossing to the sideboard, he took a number of oranges from a bowl of fruit, dropped them in the towel and pulled up its ends to form a bag. He came toward her, swinging it loosely. Again, Lilly tried to brace herself with limpness.

She knew *the oranges*. She knew all such gimmicks, though never before had she been the victim of any. The oranges was an item from the dummy-chuckers' workbag, a frammis of the professional accident fakers.

Beaten with the fruit, a person sustained bruises far out of proportion to his actual injuries. He looked badly hurt when he was hardly hurt at all.

But he could be hurt. If he was hit hard enough and in certain areas of his body. Without feeling much pain at the time, he could have his internal organs smashed. Used in just the right way (or the wrong way), the oranges produced much the same effect as an enema or douche of plaster-of-paris.

Bobo drew closer. He stopped in front of her. He moved to one side and a little behind her.

He gripped the towel with both hands. And swung.

And let the oranges spill harmlessly to the floor.

He gestured.

She bent to pick up the fruit. And then again she was sprawling. And his knees were in her back and his hand was against her head. And she was pinned, spreadeagled, against the carpet.

A couple passed in the hallway, laughing and talking. A couple from another planet. From the dining room – from another world – came the faint sound of music.

There was the click of a cigarette lighter, the smell of smoke. Then, the smell of burning flesh as he held the glowing coal against the back of her right hand. He held it with measured firmness, just enough to keep it burning without crushing it out.

His knees worked with expert cruelty.

The cigarette burned into her hand, and his knees probed the sensitive nerves of her spine.

It was a timeless world, an endless hell. There was no escape from it. There was no relief in it. She couldn't cry out. It was impossible even to squirm. The world was at once to be endured and unendurable. And the one possible relief was within her own small body.

Scalding urine spurted from her loins. It seemed to pour from her in a flood.

And Bobo stood up, releasing her, and she got up and went into the bathroom.

She held her hand under the ice-water tap, then patted it with a towel and examined it. The burn was ugly, but it didn't appear to be serious. None of the large veins were affected. She lowered her slacks and swabbed herself with a slightly moistened towel. That was about as much as could be done here. The raincoat would cover up her stained clothes.

She left the bathroom, crossed to the lounge where Bobo was seated, and accepted the drink he gave her. He took out his wallet. and extended a thick sheaf of new bills.

'Your five grand, Lilly. I almost forgot.'

'Thanks, Bo.'

'How you making out these days, anyway? Stealing much from me?'

'Not much. My folks didn't raise any stupid kids,' Lilly said. 'I just clip a buck here and a buck there. It mounts up, but nobody gets hurt.'

'That's right,' Justus nodded approvingly. 'Take a little, leave a little.'

'I look on it this way,' Lilly said, shrewdly enunciating his own philosophy. 'A person that don't look out for himself is too dumb to look out for anyone else. He's a liability, right, Bo?'

'Absolutely! You're a thousand per cent right, Lil!'

'Or else he's working an angle. If hc doesn't steal a little, he's stealing big.'

'Right!'

'I like that suit, Bo. I don't know what there is about it, but somehow it makes you look so much taller.'

'Yeah?' He beamed at her. 'You really think so? You know a lot of people been telling me the same thing.'

Their amiable talk continued as twilight slid into the room. And Lilly's hand ached, and the wet clothes burned and chafed her flesh. She had to leave him feeling good about her. She had to make sure that the score between them was settled, and that he was actually letting her off so lightly.

They discussed several business matters she had handled for him in Detroit and the Twin Cities on her circuitous way to the coast. Bobo revealed that he was only in town for the day. Tomorrow he was heading back east via Vegas, Galveston, and Miami.

'Another drink, Lilly?'

'Well, just a short one. I've got to be running along pretty soon.'

'What's the hurry? I thought maybe we could have dinner together.'

'I'd like to, but . . .'

It was best not to stay, best to quit while she was ahead. She'd been very, very lucky apparently, but luck could run out on you.

'I've got a son living here, Bo. A salesman. I don't get to see him very often, so . . .'

'Well, sure, sure,' he nodded. 'How's he making out?'

'He's in the hospital. Some kind of stomach trouble. I usually visit him every night.'

'Sure, naturally,' he frowned. 'Gettin' everything he needs? Anything I can do?'

Lilly thanked him, shaking her head. 'He's doing fine. I think he'll be getting out in a day or two.'

'Well, you'd better run along,' Bobo said. 'A boy's sick, he wants his mother.'

She got the raincoat out of the closet, and belted it around her. They said good night, and she left.

A little urine had trickled down her legs, making them itch and sting, and leaving an unpleasant sogginess in her shoes. Her underpants chafed and stung, and the seat of the slacks seemed to have soaked through. The ache in her right hand grew, spread slowly up into her wrist and arm.

She hoped she hadn't soiled Bobo's lounge. She'd been very lucky, considering the amount her blunder must have cost him, but a little thing like that might spoil it.

She picked up her car, and drove away from the hotel.

As she entered her apartment, she kicked out of her shoes, began flinging her clothes from her; leaving them in a trail behind her as she hurried toward the bathroom. She closed its door. Kneeling, she went down in front of the toilet as though it were an altar, and a great sob shook her body.

Weeping hysterically, laughing and crying, she began to vomit.

Lucky . . .
Got off easy . . .
Boy, am I lucky!

10

At a few minutes before noon, Moira Langtry came out of the arched door of the hospital and crossed the street to the parking lot. She'd risen unusually early that day in order to turn herself out with extra care, and the result was all that she could have hoped for. She was a brunette dream, a fragrant sultry-eyed vision of loveliness. The nurses had looked after her enviously as she tripped down the corridor. The doctors and interns had almost drooled, their eyes lingering on the delicate shivering of her breasts and the sensual swing of her rounded little hips.

Women almost always disliked Moira. She was glad that they did, taking it as a compliment and returning their dislike. Men, of course, were invariably drawn to her, a reaction which she expected and cultivated but was emotionally cold to. Very rarely did they appeal to her. Roy Dillon was one of the rare ones who did. In her own way, she had been faithful to him during the three years of their acquaintance.

Roy was fun. Roy stirred her. Man-wise, he was the luxury which she had clutched to herself no more than a half-dozen times in her life. Six men out of the hundreds who had had her body.

If she could put him to practical use, fine. She hoped and believed she could do just that. If not, she still wanted him, and she did not intend to have him taken from her. It wasn't, of course, that she absolutely couldn't do without him; women who got that way over a man were strictly for the movies. But she simply couldn't afford such a loss, its clear threat to her security.

When things reached the point where she couldn't hold a man, then she was finished. She might as well do a high brodie out of the nearest window.

So today she had risen early, knocking herself out to be a knockout. Thinking that by arriving at the hospital at an off-hour, she could see Roy alone for a change and tease his appetite for what he had been missing. It was highly necessary, she felt. Particularly with his mother working against her, and throwing that cute little nurse at him.

And today, after all the trouble she'd gone to, his damned snotty mother was there. It was almost as though Mrs Dillon had read her mind, intuitively suspecting her visit to the hospital and busting her goddamned pants to be there at the same time.

Smoldering, Moira reached the parking lot. The pimply-faced attendant hastened to open the door of her car, and as she climbed into it, she rewarded him with a look at her legs.

She drove off the lot, breathing heavily, wishing that she could get Lilly Dillon alone in a good dark alley. The more she thought about her recent visit the angrier she became.

That's what you got for trying to be nice to people! You tried to be nice to 'em and they made you look like a fool!

'Please don't tell me that I can't really be Roy's mother, Mrs Langtry. I'm rather tired of hearing it.'

'Sorry! I didn't mean it, of course. You're about fifty, Mrs Dillon?'

'Just about, dear. Just about your own age.'

'I think I'd better leave!'

'I can give you a lift, if you like. It's only a Chrysler convertible, but it probably beats riding a bus.'

'Thanks! I have my bicycle with me.'

'Lilly. Mrs Langtry drives a Cadillac.'

'Not really! But don't you think they're rather common, Mrs Langtry? I know they're a very good car, but it seems like every overdressed hustler you see these days is driving a Cadillac.'

Moira's hands tightened on the wheel of the car.

She told herself that she could cheerfully kill Mrs Dillon. She could strangle her with her bare hands.

At her apartment house, she turned the Cadillac over to the doorman, and went on through the lobby to the grill and cocktail lounge.

It was well into the noon-hour now. Many of the tables were occupied, and waiters in smart white pea jackets were hurrying in and out of the kitchen with trays of delicately smelling food. One of them brought Moira an outsize menu. She studied it, hesitating over the filet mignon sandwich with stuffed mushrooms (6.75).

She was hungry. Breakfast had consisted of her usual unsweetened grapefruit and black coffee. But she needed a drink more than she needed food: two or three strong, reassuring drinks. And she could allow herself only so many calories a day.

Closing the menu, she handed it back to the waiter. 'Just a drink now, Allen,' she smiled. 'I'll eat later on.'

'Certainly, Mrs Langtry. A martini, perhaps? Gibson?'

'Mmm, no. Something with a little more character, I

believe. A sidecar, say, with bourbon instead of brandy. And, Allen, no Triple Sec, please.'

'Emphatically!' The waiter wrote on his pad. 'We always use Cointreau in a sidecar. Now, would you like the rim of the glass sugared or plain?'

'Plain. About an ounce and a half of bourbon to an ounce of Cointreau, and a twist of lime peel instead of lemon.'

'Right away, Mrs Langtry.'

'And, Allen . . .'

'Yes, Mrs Langtry?'

'I want that served in a champagne glass. A thoroughly chilled glass, please.'

'Certainly.'

Moira watched him as he hurried away, her carefully composed features concealing an incipient snicker. Now, wasn't that something, she thought. No wonder the world was going to hell when a grown man pranced around in a monkey suit, brown-nosing dames who made a big deal out of ordering a belt of booze! Where had it all started? she wondered. Where the beginning of this detour which had sidetracked civilization into mixing drinks with one hand and stirring up bombs with the other?

She thought about it, not thinking in those words, of course. Simply feeling that the times were out of joint with themselves, and that the most emphasis was put on the least-worthwhile pursuits.

What it all boiled down to really was everybody giving everybody else a hard time for no good reason whatever. And the hell of it was that there seemed to be no way of getting on the right track. You couldn't be yourself any-more. If a woman ordered a straight double-shot with a beer chaser in a place like this, they'd probably throw her out. Ditto, if she asked for a hamburger with raw onions.

You just couldn't march to your own music. Nowadays, you couldn't even hear it . . . She could no longer hear it. It was lost, the music which each person had inside himself, and which put him in step with things as they should be. Lost along with the big, bluff man, the joking introspective man, who had taught her how to listen for it.

Cole Langley (Lindsey, Lonsdale). Cole 'The Farmer' Langley.

Her drink came, and she took a quick sip of it. Then, with a touch of desperation, she half-emptied the glass. That helped. She could think of Cole without wanting to break up.

She and The Farmer had lived together for ten years, ten of the most wonderful years of her life. It had been a kind of camping-out-living, the kind that most people would turn up their noses at, but it was that way by choice not necessity. With Cole, it seemed the only possible way to live.

They always traveled by chair-car in those days. They wore whatever they felt like wearing, usually overalls or khakis for him and gingham for her. When it was possible to obtain, Cole would have a two-quart jar of corn whiskey in a paper sack. Instead of eating in diners, they carried a huge lunch wrapped in newspapers. And every time the train stopped, Cole would hop off and buy gobs of candy and cold drinks and cookies and everything else he could lay hands on.

They couldn't begin to eat so much themselves, naturally. Cole gloried in abundance, but he was a rather finicky eater and a very light drinker. The food and the booze were to pass around, and the way he did it no one ever refused. He knew just the right thing to say to each person – a line of scripture, a quote from Shakespeare, a homely joke. Before they'd been in the car an hour, everyone was eating and drinking and warming up to everyone else. And Cole would be beaming on them as though they were a bunch of kids and he was a doting father.

Women didn't hate her in those days.

Men didn't look at her the way they did now.

Friendliness, the ability to make friends, was The Farmer's stock in trade, of course. Something eventually to be cashed in on through small-town banks via a series of simple-seeming but bewildering maneuvers. But he insisted on regarding the payoffs as no more than a fair exchange. For mere money, a thing useless and meaningless in itself, he traded great hopes and a new perspective on life. And nothing was ever managed so that the frammis would show through for what it was. Always the people were left with hope and belief.

What more could they want, anyway? What could be more important in life than having something to hope for and something to believe in?

For more than a year, they lived on a rundown farm in Missouri, a rocky clay-soiled sixty acres with a completely unmodernized house and an outdoor privy. That was their best time together.

It was a two-hole privy, and sometimes they'd sit together in it for hours. Peering out at the occasional passersby on the rutted red-clay road. Watching the birds hop about in the yard. Talking quietly or reading from the stack of old newspapers and magazines that cluttered one corner of the building.

'Now, look at this, Moira,' he would say, pointing to an advertisement. 'While the price of steak has gone up twenty-three cents a pound in the last decade, the price of coal has only advanced one and one-half cents per pound. It looks like the coal dealers are giving us quite a break, doesn't it?'

'Well . . .' She didn't always know how to respond to him; whether he was just making an idle comment or telling her something.

'Or maybe they aren't either,' he'd say, 'when you consider that meat is normally sold by the pound and coal by the ton.'

Now and then, she'd come up with just the right answer, like the time he'd pointed out that 'four out of five doctors' took aspirin, and what did she think about that, anyway?

'I'd say the fifth doctor was a lucky guy,' she said. 'He's the only one who doesn't have headaches.' And Cole had been very pleased with her.

They got a lot of fun out of the advertisements. For years afterward, she could look at some nominally straightforward pronouncement and break into laughter.

Beware the wiry zone . . . Are germs lurking in your nooks and crannies? . . . You, too, can learn to dance!

Even now she laughed over them. But wryly, with sardonic bitterness. Not as she and Cole Langley had laughed.

One day, when he was trying to dig down to the bottom of the magazine pile, it toppled over, uncovering a small box-like structure with a hole cut in the top. A kid's toilet.

Moira had made some comment about its being cute. But Cole went on staring at it, the laughter dying in his eyes, his mouth loosening sickishly. Then he turned and whispered to her:

'I'll bet they killed the kid. I'll bet it's buried down there under us . . .'

She was stunned, speechless. She sat staring at him, unable to move or speak, and Cole seemed to take her silence for agreement. He went on talking, low-voiced, even more impellingly persuasive than he normally was. And after a time, there was no reality but the hideousness he created, and she found herself nodding to what he said.

No, no child should be allowed to live. Yes, all children should be killed at birth or as soon afterward as possible. It was the kindest thing to do. It was the only way to spare them the futile torment, the frustrating and senseless torture, the paradoxically evil mess which represented life on the planet Earth.

Subconsciously, she knew she was seeing him for the first time, and that the laughing, gregarious Cole was only a shadow fleeing its owner's convictions. Subconsciously, she wanted to scream that he was wrong, that there were no absolutes of any kind, and that the real man might well be fleeing the shadow.

But she lacked the vocabulary for such thoughts, the mentality to string them together. They wandered about in her subconscious, unguided and uncohered, while Cole, as always, was utterly convincing. So, in the end, she had been persuaded. She agreed with everything he said.

And suddenly he had started cursing her. So she was a faker, too! A stinking hypocrite! She could do nothing for herself and nothing for anyone else because she believed in nothing.

From that day on The Farmer was on the toboggan. They jumped from the sticks to St Louis, and when he wasn't dead drunk he was shooting himself full of hop.

They had a hefty hunk of loot – rather Moira had it. Secretly, in the way of many wives – although she was not legally his wife – she had been rat-holing money for years. But the substantial sum she had cached wouldn't last a month at the rate he was going, so, as she saw it, there was only one thing to do. She took up hustling.

There was no stigma attached to it in their professional circle. In fact, it was an accepted practice for a woman to prostitute herself when her man was low on his back. But whores *per se* were a dime a dozen, and only girls with 'class,' the expensively turned-out dames, could pull down the big money. And Cole was infuriated by a classy Moira.

He grew fanatical in his charges that she was a hypocrite and 'unbeliever,' shouting down her pleas that she wished only to help him. Wildly, he declared that she was a whore at heart, that she had always been a whore, that she had been one when he met her.

That was not true. In her early working life, as a photographer's model and cocktail waitress, she had occasionally given herself to men and received gifts in return. But it wasn't the same as whoring. She had liked the men involved. What she gave them was given freely, without bargaining, as were their gifts to her.

So Cole's false charges, insensibly made though they were, began to hurt more and more. Perhaps he didn't know what he was saying, or perhaps he did. But even the innocent blow of a child can be painful, possibly more so than that of an adult since its victim cannot bring himself to strike back. His only recourse, when the pain becomes unbearable, is to put himself beyond the child's reach . . .

Moira's last memory of Cole 'The Farmer' Langley was that of a wildly weeping man in overalls, shouting 'Whore!'

from the curb in front of their swank apartment house as a grinning cab-driver drove her away.

She wanted to leave the rat-holed money for him. Or half of it, at least. But she knew it was useless. It would either be stolen from him, or he would throw it away. He was beyond help – her help, in any event – and anything she might do would only prolong his agony.

What had happened to him, she didn't know. Deliberately, she had tried to avoid knowing. But she hoped that he was dead. It was the best she could hope for the man she had loved so much.

11

Moira took a long sip of her third bourbon sidecar. Feeling just a little skittish (she had a horror of actual drunkenness), she grinned at the man who was approaching her table.

His name was Grable, Charles Grable, and he was the manager of the apartment house. Dressed in striped trousers and a black broadcloth morning coat, he had rather close-set eyes and a plump, peevish-looking face. His attempt to look stern, as he sat down, gave his small mouth a baby-like pout.

'Don't tell me, now,' Moira said, solemnly. 'You're Addison Simms of Seattle, and we had lunch together in the fall of 1902.'

'What? What are you talking about?' Grable snapped. 'Now, you listen to me, Moira! I – '

'How is your wiry zone?' Moira said. 'Are hidden germs lurking in your nooks and crannies?'

'Moira!' He leaned forward angrily, dropping his voice. 'I'm telling you for the last time, Moira. I want your bill settled today! Every last penny of it, your rent and all the other charges you've run up! You either pay it, or I'm locking you out of your apartment!'

'Now, Charles. Don't I always pay my bills? Aren't they always settled . . . one way or another?'

Grable flushed, and looked over his shoulder. A half-pleading, half-whining note came into his voice.

'I can't do that any more, Moira. I simply can't! People staying over their leases, coming in ahead of their lease-dates – paying money that I don't show on the books! I – I – '

'I understand.' Moira gave him a sad. sultry look. 'You just don't like me any more.'

'No, no that's not it at all! I – '

'You don't either,' she pouted. 'If you did, you wouldn't act this way.'

'I told you I couldn't help it! I – I – ' He saw the lurking mockery in her eyes. 'All right!' he snarled. 'Laugh at me, but you're not making a thief out of me any longer. You're nothing but a cheap little – little – '

'Cheap, Charles? Now, I didn't think I was at all cheap.'

'I'm through talking,' he said firmly. 'Either you settle up by five o'clock tonight or out you go, and I'll hold on to every thing you own!'

He stamped away with a kind of furtive indignation.

Moira shrugged indifferently, and picked up her drink. He's a secret sufferer, she told herself. *Stop getting up nights, men!*

She signaled for her check, penciled on a dollar tip for the waiter. As he nodded gracefully, pulling back her chair, she told him that he, too, could learn to dance.

'All you need is the magic step,' she said. 'It's as simple as one-two-three.'

He laughed politely. Cloud-nine kidding was old stuff in a place like this. 'Like some coffee before you leave, Mrs Langtry?'

84

'Thank you, no,' Moira smiled. 'The drinks were very good, Allen.'

She left the lounge, and passed back through the lobby. Recovering her car, she headed toward the downtown business district.

All things considered, she had lived quite economically since her arrival in Los Angeles. Economically, that is, insofar as her own money was concerned. Of the boodle with which she had skipped St Louis, she still had several thousand dollars, plus, of course, such readily negotiable items as her car, jewelry, and furs. But lately, she had had an increasingly strong hunch that her life here was drawing to a close, and that it was time to cash in wherever and whatever she could.

She hated to leave the city; particularly hated the idea that it would mean giving up Roy Dillon. But it didn't necessarily have to mean that, and if it did, well, it just couldn't be helped. Hunches were to be heeded. You did what you had to do.

Arriving downtown, she parked the car on a privately-operated lot. It was owned by a better-class jewelry store, one which she had patronized both as a buyer and seller, though largely the last. The doorman touched his cap and swung open the plate-glass doors for her, and one of the junior executives came forward, smiling.

'Mrs Langtry, how nice to see you again! Now, how can we serve you today?'

Moira told him. He nodded gravely, and led her back to a small private office. Closing the door, he seated her at the desk and sat down opposite her.

Moira took a bracelet from her purse, and handed it to him. His eyes widened appreciatively.

'Beautiful,' he murmured, reaching for a loupe. 'A wonderful piece of workmanship. Now, let's just see . . .'

Moira watched him, as he snapped on a gooseneck lamp, and turned the bracelet in his clean, strong hands. He had waited on her several times before. He wasn't handsome; almost homely, in fact. But she liked him, and she knew that he was strongly attracted to her.

He let the loupe drop from his eye, shook his head with genuine regret.

'I can't understand a thing like this,' he said. 'It's something you almost never see.'

'How . . . what do you mean?' Moira frowned.

'I mean this is some of the finest filigreed platinum I've ever seen. Practically a work of art. But the stones, no. They're not diamonds, Mrs Langtry. Excellent imitations, but still imitations.'

Moira couldn't believe him. Cole had paid four thousand dollars for the bracelet.

'But they must be diamonds! They cut glass!'

'Mrs Langtry,' he smiled wryly, 'glass will cut glass. Practically anything will. Let me show you a positive test for diamonds.'

He handed her the loupe, and took an eyedropper from his desk. Carefully, he dropped a miniscule amount of water on the stones.

'Do you see how the water splashes over them, slides off in a sheet? With real diamonds it won't do that. It clings to the surface in tiny droplets.'

Moira nodded dully, and took the loupe from her eye.

'Do you happen to know where it was purchased, Mrs Langtry? I'm sure your money could be recovered.'

She didn't know. Quite possibly Cole had bought it as a fake. 'It isn't worth anything to you?'

'Why, of course it is,' he said warmly. 'I can offer you – well, five hundred dollars?'

'Very well. If you'll give me a check, please.'

He excused himself, and left for several minutes. He returned with the check, placed it in an envelope for her and sat down again.

'Now,' he said, 'I hope you're not too badly disappointed with us. You'll give us an opportunity to serve you again, I hope.'

Moira hesitated. She glanced at the small sign on his desk. *Mr Carter.* The store was named Carter's. The owner's son, perhaps?

'I should have told you, Mrs Langtry. With a valued customer, such as you, we'd be very happy to call at your home. It's not at all necessary for you to come to the store. If there's anything you think we might be interested in . . .'

'I have only one thing, Mr Carter.' Moira looked at him evenly. '*Are* you interested?'

'Well. I'd have to see it, of course. But – '

'You are seeing it, Mr Carter. You're looking right at it.'

He looked puzzled, then startled. Then, his face assumed something of the same expression it had worn when he was examining the bracelet.

'You know something, Mrs Langtry? A bracelet like the one you sold us, we seldom run across anything like that. A fine setting and workmanship are usually indicative of precious stones. It always hurts me when I find they're not. I always hope' – he raised his eyes – 'that I'm mistaken.'

Moira smiled, liking him better than ever.

'At this point,' she said, 'I think I should say ouch.'

'Say it for both of us, Mrs Langtry,' he laughed. 'This is one of those times when I almost wish I wasn't married. Almost.'

They walked to the entrance together, the lovely smartly-dressed woman and the homely, clean-looking young man. As they said good-bye, he held her hand for a moment.

'I hope everything straightens out for you, Mrs Langtry. I do wish I could have helped.'

'Just stay in there and pitch,' Moira told him. 'You're on the right team.'

Very hungry by now, she had coffee and a small salad at a drugstore. Then, she returned to her apartment house.

The manager was on the lookout for her, and he was knocking at her door almost as soon as she had closed it. Curtly, he thrust an itemized bill at her. Moira examined it, her eyebrows raising now and then.

'A lot of money, Charles,' she murmured. 'You wouldn't have padded it a little, would you?'

'Don't you talk to me that way! You owe every doggone cent of it and you know it, and by golly you're going to pay it!'

'Maybe I could get the dough from your wife, do you suppose, Charlie? Maybe your kiddies would crack their piggy banks?'

'You leave them out of this! You go near my family, and I'll – I'll – ' His voice broke into a pleading whine. 'Y-you . . . you wouldn't do that, would you, Moira?'

Moira gave him a disgusted look. 'Oh, don't wet your pants, for God's sake! Mark the damned bill paid, and I'll get you the money.'

She turned abruptly and entered her bedroom. Opening her purse, she took out a roll of bills and dropped it on the dressing table. Then, as she undressed swiftly, slipping into a sheer black negligee, her weary frown suddenly broke and she snickered.

Laughing silently, she spread herself out on the bed.

She often broke into sudden fits of merriment. Faced with some unpleasant facet of the present, she would force her mind away from it, letting it wander vagrantly until it seized upon some ridiculous parallel or paradox. And then, for no apparent reason, she laughed.

Now, the laughter became briefly audible, and Grable called to her suspiciously from the vicinity of the doorway.

'What are you up to, Moira? What are you laughing about?'

'You wouldn't understand, Charles; just a little item from the luncheon menu. Come on in.'

He came in. He looked at her and gulped, then frantically pulled his gaze away.

'I want that m-money, Moira! I want it right now!'

'Well, there it is.' The negligee fell open as she waved a bare foot at the dresser. 'There's the money, and here's little Moira.'

He strode toward the dressing table. Just before he reached it, his step faltered and he turned slowly around.

'Moira, I – I –' He stared at her, gulping again, licking back the sudden saliva from the corners of his babyish mouth. And this time he could not pull his eyes away.

Moira looked down at herself, following the course of his gaze.

'The automatic clutch, Charles,' she murmured. 'It comes with the de luxe upholstery and the high-speed wiry zone.'

He made a little rush toward her. He stopped weakly, a hand held out in wretched appeal.

'P-please, Moira! Please, *please*! I've been good to you! I've let you stay h-here month after month, and . . . You will, won't you? Just – '

Moira said, nope, it couldn't be done. All passengers must pay as they entered, and no free passes or rebates. 'That's a strict rule of the Intercourse Commerce Commission, Charles. All common carriers are governed by it.'

'Please! You got to! *You j-just got to!*' Almost sobbing, he sagged down on his knees at the side of the bed. 'Oh, God, God, God! D-don't make me – '

'Only one choice to a customer,' Moira said firmly. 'The lady or the loot. So what's it going to be?' And then, as he abruptly flung himself at her, 'As if I didn't know . . .'

She lay looking up past his shoulder, trying to blot out his panting, thrusting presence. Forcing her mind away from him and to

Roy Dillon. Their last afternoon at the hotel. Why his sudden hemorrhage, anyway, a young guy with an apparently cast-iron stomach? What had happened to bring it on? Or was it really on the level? Could it be some angle his mother was working to break them up?

She looked like an angle-player! Plenty like one! You could see that she was sharp as a tack and twice as hard – anyone could see it that knew their way around. And she was loaded with dough, and . . .

Moira didn't want to think about her, the snotty little witch! Anything else, but not her! She'd like to *do* something about her, but –

She rolled her eyes at the ceiling. What a character this guy was! What a revolting character! He must be wearing forty dollars' worth of toilet water and hair gook, but it didn't really touch him. It was just sort of wrapped around him, like foil around a chunk of limburger, and when you got down under it –

Ooops! She tightened her lips quickly, her cheeks bulging with repressed merriment. She tried to jerk her mind away from its source, from that darned crazy menu. But it just wouldn't go away, and again she was shaking with laughter.

'Whassa matter?' gasped Grable. 'How can you laugh at a – '

'Nothing. N-never mind, Charles. I j-just – ah, ha, ha, ha – I'm s-sorry, but – ahh, ha, his ha . . .'

Luncheon Special. Broiled hothouse tomato under generous slice of ripe cheese.

12

illy Dillon's apartment was on the top floor of a Sunset Strip building a few blocks east of the city limits of Beverly Hills. Rented furnished, it consisted of a bedroom, bath, powder room, kitchen, living room, and den. The den was on the rear or south side of the building, and a hospital bed had been put into it for Roy. He lay on it today, in pajamas and bathrobe, its head cranked up so that he could look out over unlimited miles of oil fields, ocean, and beach towns.

He felt lazy and comfortable. He felt restless and guilty. This was the beginning of his third week out of the hospital. He was fully recovered, and there was no valid excuse for his remaining here. And yet he lingered on. Lilly wanted him to. The doctors passively encouraged him to, seeing little to be gained by his protracted convalescence but a broad margin of safety in it.

The ruptured vessels of his stomach *could* open up again, under just the right circumstances. They *could* be re-ruptured. Thus, if he wished to remain completely inactive and beyond reach of the smallest risk, it was quite agreeable with the doctors.

Aside from Lilly and the matter of his health, Roy had

another reason for staying on. A guilty reason, and one he tried not to admit to. She, Carol Roberg, was in the kitchen now, cleaning up their luncheon dishes and doubtless preparing a dessert for them. He didn't want any himself – he had gained almost seven pounds in the past two weeks – but he knew that she did. And not for the world would he have interfered.

Carol was very dainty about her eating, as she was about everything. But he had never seen anyone who could stow away so much food so quickly.

He wondered about that, her insatiable appetite, when he was not wondering about her in a different way. Most women he knew seemed hardly to eat anything. Moira, for example . . .

Moira . . .

He squirmed uneasily as he recalled her visit this morning. He had told her yesterday in a subdued telephone conversation that Lilly was leaving the apartment early today, and suggested that she drop by. So she had come, pulling up startled when she saw Carol, then giving him a quick, questioning look.

Carol sat down in the living room with them. She apparently felt that it was only polite to do so, and she tried to make conversation about the weather and the usual routine topics. When, after what was probably the longest half-hour on record, she had finally excused herself and gone into the kitchen, Moira turned on him, tightmouthed.

'I tried to send her out,' Roy said helplessly. 'I told her to take off a few hours.'

'*Tried* to? If it were me, you'd just said to beat it.'

'I'm sorry,' he said. 'I wanted to be alone as much as you did.'

He glanced quickly over his shoulder, then went down beside her chair and took her into his arms. She submitted to a kiss, but there was no response to it. He kissed her again, letting his hands rove over her body, probing the soft, sweet-scented curves. After weeks of enforced continence, and the constant temptation which Carol represented, he had never wanted Moira as much as he did at that moment. But abruptly she had pulled away from him.

'Just how much longer do you plan on staying here, Roy?' she asked. 'When are you moving back to the hotel?'

'Well. I don't know exactly. Pretty soon, I imagine.'

'You're not in much of a hurry, are you? You like it here.'

Roy said awkwardly that he had no complaints. He was being well taken care of – much better than he could be in a hotel – and Lilly was anxious to have him stay.

'Mmm, I'll bet she is, and I'll bet you're darned well taken care of, too!'

'What do you mean?'

'Are you kidding? I've seen the way you looked at that simpering little simp of a nurse! Either you're losing your grip, or you think she's too good to tumble. She is, but I'm not!'

'Oh, for God's sake . . .' He reddened. 'Look, I'm sorry about today. If there was any way I could get rid of her without hurting her feelings . . .'

'Naturally, you couldn't do that. Oh, no!'

'Let's just say that I wouldn't do it then,' he said, tiring of apology.

'Well, forget it.' She picked up her gloves, and stood up. 'If it suits you, it suits me.'

He followed her out into the hallway, trying to smooth over the rift without unbending too far. Liking her, desiring her more than he ever had, yet wary as always of any tightening of her hold upon him.

'I'll be out of here any day, now,' he assured her. 'I'm probably a hell of a lot more anxious than you are.'

'Well . . .' She smiled tentatively, the dark eyes searching his face. 'I'm not so sure of that.'

'You'll see. Maybe we can go to La Jolla this weekend.'

'Just maybe?'

'I'm practically sure of it,' he said. 'I'll give you a ring, hmm?'

So he had got things straightened out, for a time, at least, and after a fashion. But he had gotten nothing in return, nothing but the status quo, and unsatisfied desire squirmed in him relentlessly. Something was going to have to give, he told himself. With Moira's presence still lingering with him, with Carol so readily accessible . . .

Carol. He wondered just what he should do about her anyway. Or whether he should do anything about her. She looked completely virginal, and if she was, that was that. She'd remain that way, as far as he was concerned. But looks could be deceptive; and sometimes, when she consented to a kiss and she clung to him for a moment, well, he wasn't so sure about her status. Was, in fact, almost positive that he had judged it wrongly.

And in that case, of course . . .

She came in from the kitchen, bearing two cream-topped parfait glasses. He accepted one of them, and she sat down with the other. Smiling, he watched as she dipped into it, wanting to sweep her up in his arms and give her a hearty squeeze.

'Good?' he said.

'Wonderful!' she exclaimed enthusiastically. Then, looking up at him, pinking with self-consciousness. 'All the time here, I am eating! You think I am such a pig, yes?'

Roy laughed. 'If they made pigs like you, I'd start raising them. How about eating mine, too?'

'But it is yours. More I could not possibly eat!'

'Sure you can,' he said, swinging his legs off the bed. 'Will you come into the bedroom when you're through?'

'I will come now. You want your rubdown, yes?'

'No, no,' he said quickly. 'There's no hurry. Finish your ice cream first.'

He crossed the deeply carpeted living room and entered the bedroom. Entering the bedroom, he hesitated for a long moment, almost deciding to stop now while he could. Then, swiftly, before he could change his mind, he flung off the robe and his pajama top and stretched out on the bed.

Carol came in a minute or two later. She started to get the alcohol bottle from the bathroom, and he held out his hand to her.

'Come here, Carol. I want to ask you something.'

She nodded, and sat down on the edge of the bed. He drew her closer, bringing her face down to his; and, then, as their lips met, he began to draw her prone.

Nervously her body suddenly stiffening, she tried to pull away. 'Oh, no! Please, Roy. I – I – '

'It's all right. I want to ask you something, Carol. Will you tell me the truth?'

'Well' – she tried to muster a smile. 'It is so important to you? Or perhaps you are teasing me again, yes?'

'It's very important to me,' he said. 'Are you a virgin, Carol?'

The smile washed abruptly from her face, and for a moment it was something completely blank. Then, a trace of color came back into it and her eyes fell, and almost imperceptibly she shook her head.

'No, I am not a virgin.'

'You're not?' He was vaguely disappointed.

'I am not. Not by many times.' Under its surface firmness, her voice shook slightly. 'And now you will not like me any more.'

'Not like you? Why, of course, I do. I like you more than ever!'

'B-but – ' She smiled tremulously, began to glow with a kind of joyous incredulity. 'You really mean it? You would not tease about so important a thing?'

'What's so important about it? Now, come on, honey!'

Laughing joyously, she allowed him to pull her down against him; hugged him with laughing wonderment. Oh, my, she said. She was so happy. And then, with no real resistance, bubbling with the happiness, he had given her, 'But – shouldn't we wait, Roy? You would not like me better?'

'I couldn't like you any better!' He tugged impatiently at her white uniform. 'How do you get this damned thing – ?'

'But there is something else you must know. You have a right to know. I – I cannot have children, Roy. Never.'

That stopped him, made him hesitate, but only for a second. She had an awkward way of phrasing things, twisting them around hindside-to and putting the emphasis in the wrong places. So she couldn't have children and that was all to the good, but he would have taken care of that, anyway.

'Who cares?' he said, almost groaning in his hunger for her. 'It's okay and it's okay if you're not a virgin. Now, can't you stop talking, for God's sake, and – '

'Yes! Oh, yes, Roy!' She clung to him in wondrous surrender, guiding his fumbling hands. 'Also, I want to. And it is your right . . .'

The uniform fell away from her; the underthings. The innate modesty, the fears, the past. In the drape-drawn dimness of the room, she was reborn. and there was no past but only a future.

The purplish brand still lingered on her outflung left arm, but now it was merely a childhood scar; time dulled, shrunken by growth. It didn't matter. What it memorialized didn't matter – the sterilization, the loss of virginity – for he had said it didn't. So the thing itself was without meaning: the indelible imprint of the Dachau concentration camp.

13

She came out of the bathroom, modestly wearing her underthings now; still flushed and warm and glowing. Primly protective, she drew up the sheet and tucked it over his chest. 'I must take care of you,' she said. 'Now, more than ever, you are most important to me.'

Roy grinned at her lazily. She was sweet, a lot of woman, he thought. And about the most honest one he'd ever met. If she hadn't told him that she wasn't virginal . . .

'You are all right, Roy? You do not hurt any place?'

'I never felt better in my life,' he laughed. 'Not that I haven't been feeling okay.'

'That is good. It would be terrible if I had given you hurt.'

He repeated that he was feeling fine; she was just what he'd needed. She said seriously that she also had needed him, and he laughed again, winking at her.

'I believe you, honey. How long has it been, anyway, or shouldn't I ask?'

'How long?' She frowned a little, her head tilted in puzzlement. Then, 'Oh,' she said. 'Well, it – it was –'

'Never mind,' he said quickly. 'Forget it.'

'It was there.' She extended the tattooed arm. 'There also I was made sterile.'

'There?' he frowned. 'I don't . . . What's that, anyway?'

She explained absently, her smile fixing; the tilted-up eyes looking at him and through him toward something far, beyond. Seemingly, she was speaking of the abstract, a dull and tenuous theorem scarcely worthy of recital. Seemingly, she was reading from a fairy tale, a thing so filled with terrors that they clung stagnating to one another; never advancing the plot or theme, physically motionless, merely horror piled upon horror until they sagged slowly downward, drawing the listener with them.

'Yes, yes, that is right.' She smiled at him as though at a precocious child. 'Yes, I was very young, seven or eight, I think. That was the reason, you see: to discover the earliest possible age at which a female might conceive. It can be very early in life, as young as five, I think. But an average minimum age was being sought. With my mother and grandmother, it was the other way; I mean, how old could the female be. My grandmother died shortly after the beginning of the experiment, but my mother . . .'

Roy wanted to vomit. He wanted to shake her, to beat her. Standing apart from himself, as she was standing from herself, he was furious with her. Subjectively, his thoughts were not a too-distant parallel of the current popular philosophizing. The things you heard and read and saw everywhere. The pious mourning of sin; the joyous absolution of the sinners; the uncomfortable frowns and glances-askance at those who recalled their misdeeds. After all, the one-time enemies, poor fellows, were now our friends and it was bad taste to show gas-stoves on television. After all, you couldn't condemn a people, could you? And what if they had done exactly that themselves? Should you make the same regrettable error? After all, they hated the reds as much as we did, they were as eager as we were to blow every stinking red in the world to hell and gone. And after all, those people, the allegedly sinned-against, had brought most of the trouble on themselves.

It was their own fault.

It was *her* own fault.

'Now, listen to me,' he broke in on her angrily. 'No, I don't want to hear any more, damnit! If you'd told me about it in the first place instead of just saying that – letting me think that – that – '

'I know,' she said. 'It was very bad of me. But I too was thinking something else.'

'Well, now,' he mumbled, 'I don't want to put you in the wrong. I like you; I think the world of you, Carol. That's why I asked you what I did, told you it was important to me. I can see now how you might have taken it the wrong way, and I wish to God there was something I could do to square things up. But – '

But why did she keep looking at him that way, smiling that totally vacant smile; waiting for him to fill the vacuum with life? He had said he was sorry, apologized for something that was partially her own fault. But still she sat there waiting. Did she seriously expect him to give up his life, the only way of life acceptable to him, merely to correct a mistake? Well, she had no right to do so! Even if he could give what she had expected and apparently still desired, he would not do it.

She was a nice girl, and it wouldn't be fair to her.

'Now, I'll tell you what,' he said, smiling ingratiatingly. 'We can't change what's already happened, so why don't we just pretend it didn't happen? How will that be, hmm? Okay? We'll just forget this, and make a brand new start?'

She looked at him silently.

'Fine,' Roy said briskly. 'That's my sweet girl. Now, I'll skim on out of here, and let you finish dressing and – and, uh . . .'

He left, pulling on his robe as he went out of the room. Returning to the den, he flopped back down on the hospital bed, stared out unseeing at the panorama to the south; still seeing the girl in the bedroom. He'd put things very badly, he guessed. His usual glibness had failed him, just when he needed it most, and he'd sounded peevish and small-time.

What had happened to him? he wondered. What had gone wrong with his pitch?

It had been an honest mistake. She'd suffered no actual loss because of it. Why couldn't he make her understand that? Why, when he could so easily pull a real swindle without a kickback?

You can't cheat an honest man, he thought. And was unreasonably irritated by the thought.

He heard her approaching, the starchy rustle of her uniform. Working up a smile, he sat up and turned around.

She was wearing her coat, a quaintly old-world garment. She was carrying her small nurse's kit.

'I am leaving now,' she said. 'Is there anything you want before I go?'

'Leaving! But – Oh, now, look,' he said winningly. 'You can't do that, you know. It's not professional. A nurse can't walk out on a patient.'

'You do not need a nurse. We both know it. At any rate, I have ceased to be a nurse to you.'

'But – but, damnit. Carol – '

She turned away from him, started for the door. He looked after her helplessly for a moment, then caught up with her and pulled her around facing him.

'Now, I'm not going to let you do this,' he said. 'There's no reason to. You need the job, and my mother and I both want you to have it. Why – '

'Let me go, please.' She pulled away from him, again moving toward the door.

Hastily, he placed himself in front of her. 'Don't,' he begged. 'If you're sore at me, okay; maybe you think you've got a right to be. But my mother's involved here. What will she think, I mean, what will I tell her when she comes home and finds you're – '

He broke off, reddening, realizing that he had sounded fearful of Lilly. A ghost of a smile touched Carol's lips.

'Your mother will be disappointed,' she said, 'but not surprised, I think. I have thought your mother did not understand you, but now I know that she does.'

Roy looked away from her. He said curtly that that wasn't what he meant at all. 'You've got some money coming to you, your wages. If you'll tell me how much . . .'

'Nothing. Your mother paid me last night.'

'All right, then, but there's still today.'

'For today, nothing. I gave nothing of value,' she said.

Roy let out an angry snort. 'Stop acting like a two-year-old kid, will you? You've got some money coming to you, and, by God, you're going to take it!' He snatched the wallet from his robe pocket, jerked out its contents and extended it toward her. 'Now, how much? What do I owe you for today?'

She looked down at the money. Carefully, shuffling

through it with a finger, she selected three bills and held them up.

'Three dollars, yes? I have heard that was the usual price.'

'You seem to know,' he snapped. 'Aah, Carol, why – '

'Thank you. It is really too much.'

She turned, crossed the carpet to the door and went out.

Roy raised his hands helplessly, and let them drop to his sides. That was that. You couldn't square a beef with a stupe.

He went into the kitchen, warmed up some coffee and drank it, standing up. Rinsing out his cup, he glanced at the clock above the stove.

Lilly would be home in a few hours. There was something he must do before she got here. It wouldn't make this Carol thing all right with her, and it would mean tipping his hand, but it had to be done. For his own sake.

Dressing and going down to the street, he was just a little rocky. But not because there was anything wrong with him, only from his long inactivity. By the time he had gotten a taxi and reached his hotel, he felt as strong as he ever had.

He was a little embarrassed by his reception at the hotel. Of course, he'd always worked to make himself likeable; that was an essential part of his front. But he was still warmed and vaguely discomfited at the way he was welcomed home (*home!*) by Simms and the owner's employees. He was glad that he didn't have to chump them; leave them up the creek, paddleless, where people who liked him were customarily left.

Flustered, he accepted their congratulations on his recovery, reassured them as to the present state of his health. He agreed with Simms that sickness came to all men, always inconveniently and unexpectedly, and that that was how the permanent waved.

At last, he escaped to his room.

He took three thousand dollars from one of the clown pictures. Then, having carefully replaced the picture on the wall, he left the hotel and went back to Lilly's apartment.

The place seemed strangely empty without Carol. Hungeringly empty as it always is when a familiar something or someone is no longer where it was. There is a haunting sense of wrongness, of things amiss. Here is a niche crying to be filled, and the one thing that will fill it will not.

Roaming restlessly from room to room, he kept listening for her, kept seeing her in his mind's eye. He could see her everywhere, the small stiffly-starched figure, the glossy tip-curling hair, the rose-and-white face, the small clean features, upturned in childlike innocence. He could hear her voice everywhere; and always he, *you*, was in what she said . . . Did he want something? Was there something she could do for him? Was he all right? He must always tell her, please, if he wanted anything.

'*You are all right, yes? It would be terrible if I had given you hurt.*'

He started to enter the bathroom, then came up short in the doorway. A towel was draped over the sink. Scrubbed, rinsed, and hung up to dry, but still faintly imbued with the yellowishness of washed-out blood.

Roy swallowed painfully. Then, he dropped it into the hamper and slammed down the lid.

The long hours dragged by, hours that had always seemed short until today.

A little after dusk, Lilly returned.

As usual, she left her troubles outside the door; came in with an expectant smile on her face.

'Why, you're all dressed! How nice,' she said. 'Where's my girl, Carol?'

'She's not here,' Roy said. 'She – '

'Oh? Well, I guess I am a little late, and of course you're all right.' She sat down, made gestures of fanning herself. 'Whew, that lousy traffic! I could make better time hopping on one foot.'

Roy hesitated, wanting to tell her, glad of anything that would let him delay.

'How's your hand, the burn?'

'Okay,' she waved it carelessly. 'It looks like I'm branded for life, but at least it learned – taught – me something. Keep away from boobs with cigars.'

'I think you should have it bandaged.'

'No can do. Have to dip in and out of my purse too much. Anyway, it's coming along all right.'

She dismissed the subject carelessly, pleased but some-what embarrassed by his unusual concern. As the room grew silent, she took a cigarette from her purse; smiled gayly, as Roy hurried to light it.

'Hey, now, it looks like I really rate around here, doesn't it? A little more of this, and – What's that?'

She looked down at the money he had dropped into her lap. Frowning, she raised her eyes.

'Three thousand dollars,' he said. 'I hope it's enough to square us up, the hospital bills and all.'

'Well, sure. But you can't – Oh,' she said tiredly. 'I guess you can, can't you? I hoped you were playing it straight, but I guess – '

'But you knew I wasn't,' Roy nodded. 'And now there's something else you've got to know. About Carol.'

14

From Sunset Strip, a muted, gradually increasing clamor floated up to Lilly's apartment, the sounds of the dinner hour and the early beginnings of the nightclubs' day. Earlier, from about four until seven, there had been the racket of the business traffic: trucks, heavy and light pickups, making their last deliveries of the day and then turning tail toward the city; passenger cars, speeding and skidding and jockeying for position as they swarmed out from town to their own duchies of Brentwood, Bel Air, and Beverly Hills. The cars were of all kinds and sizes, from hot rods on up, but there was an awesome abundance – even a predominance, at times – of the upper-bracket makes. Caught once in the Strip's traffic, Roy had examined its content and, except for two motorcycles and a Ford, he had seen nothing, for as far as he could see, but Cadillacs, Rolls-Royces, Lincolns, and Imperials.

Now, listening to the night's throbbing, Roy wished he was down there on the Strip, or practically any place but where he was. He had told Lilly about Carol as quickly as he could, anxious to get it over with. But brushed over, it had probably sounded worse than in detail. He had felt the need to go back through it again, to explain just how what had led into what. But that seemed only to worsen matters, making him appear to pose as an honest if earthy young man who had been put to shameful disadvantage by the willful stupidity of a young woman.

There was just no good way of telling the story, he guessed. There simply wasn't, despite her definite non-prudishness and the fact she had never played the role of mother, as he saw it.

He gave a start as Lilly's purse slid to the floor with a thump. He bent forward to pick it up, then settled back uneasily as he saw what had fallen from the purse – a small, silencer-equipped gun.

Her hand closed around it. She straightened again, hefting it absently. Then, seeing his unease, her mouth twisted in a tight grin.

'Don't worry, Roy. It's a temptation, I'll admit, but it would cost me my permit.'

'Well, I wouldn't want you to do that,' Roy said. 'Not after the trouble I've already caused.'

'Oh, now, you shouldn't feel that way,' Lilly said. 'You've paid your bill, haven't you? – tossed money at me like it was going out of style. You've explained and you've apologized; you didn't really do anything to explain or apologize for, did you? I was stupid. She was stupid – stupid enough to love and trust you, and to put the best possible interpretation on what you did and said. We were fools, in other words, and it's a grifter's job to take the fools.'

'Have your own way about it,' Roy snapped. 'I've apologized, done everything I can. But if you want to get nasty – '

'But I always was nasty, wasn't I? Always giving you a hard time. There was just no good in me. never ever. And you damned well couldn't miss a chance to get back at me!'

'Wh-aat?' He looked at her sharply. 'What the hell are you talking about?'

'The same thing you've spent your life brooding about and pitying yourself about, and needling me about. Because you had a hard time as a kid. Because I didn't measure up to your standards of motherhood.'

Roy blurted out surlily that she hadn't measured up to anyone else's standards, either. Then, a little shamefaced, he tacked on a half-hearted retraction. 'Now, I don't really mean that, Lilly; you just got me sore. Anyway, you've certainly done plenty out here, a lot more than I had any right to expect, and – '

'Never mind,' she cut him off. 'It wasn't enough. You've proved it wasn't. But there's a thing or two I'd like to get straight, Roy. To your way of thinking, I was a bad mother – no, I was, so let's face it. But I wonder if it occurred to you that I didn't look on myself that way at all.'

'Well . . .' He hesitated. 'Well, no, I don't suppose you did.'

'It's all a matter of comparison, right? In the good neighborhoods you were raised in, and stacked up against the other mothers you saw there, I stank. But I didn't grow up in that kind of environment, Roy. Where I was raised, a kid was lucky if he got three months of school in his life. Lucky if he didn't die of rickets or hookworm or plain old starvation, or something worse. I can't remember a day, from the time I was old enough to remember anything, that I had enough to eat and didn't get a beating . . .'

Roy lit a cigarette, glancing at her over the match; more irritated than interested in what she was saying. What did it all amount to, anyway? Maybe she'd had a tough childhood – although he'd have to take her word for that. All he knew about was his own. But having had one, and knowing how it felt, why had she handed him the same kind of deal? She knew better. She hadn't been under the same ugly social pressures that had been brought to bear on her own parents. Why, hell, she was married and living away from home at about the age he'd finished grammar school!

Something about the last thought dug into him, cut through the layered rationalizations which warmed him in their rosy glow while holding her off in outer darkness. Irritably, he wondered just how soon he could decently break out of here. That was all he wanted. Not excuses, not explanations. Because of Carol, and because he did owe Lilly *something*, he himself had been cast in the role of apologizer and explainer. And, manfully, he had accepted it. But –

He became aware at last that the room was silent. Had been silent for some time. Lilly was leaning back in her chair, looking at him with a tiredly crooked smile.

'I seem to be keeping you up,' she said. 'Why don't you just run along and leave me to stew in my sins?'

'Now, Lilly – ' He made a defensive gesture. 'You've never heard me reproach you for anything.'

'But you have plenty to reproach me for, haven't you? It was pretty lousy of me to be a child at the same time you were. To act like a child instead of a grown woman. Yes, sir, I was a real stinker not to grow up and act grown up as fast as you thought that I should.'

Roy was stung. 'What do you want me to do?' he demanded. 'Pin a halo on you? You're doing a pretty good job of that yourself.'

'And making you look like a heel at the same time, hmm? But that's the way I am, you know; the way I've always been. Always picking on poor little Roy.'

'Oh, for God's sake, Lilly – !'

'Now, I've got just one more thing to say. I don't suppose it will do any good, but I've got to say it, anyway. Get out of the grift, Roy. Get out right now, and stay out.'

'Why? Why don't you get out yourself?'

'Why?' Lilly stared at him. 'Are you seriously asking me, *why*? Why, you brainless sap, I'd be dead if I even looked like I wanted out! It's been that way since I was eighteen years old. You don't get out of things like this – you're carried out!'

Roy wet his lips nervously. Maybe she wasn't exaggerating, although it was comforting to think that she must be. But he wasn't in her league, and he never would be.

'I'm strictly short-con, Lilly,' he said. 'Nothing but small-time stuff. I can walk away from it any time I want to.'

'It won't always be small time. With you, it couldn't be. You're only twenty-five years old, and already you can lay out three grand without turning a hair. You're only twenty-five, and you've come up with a new angle on the grift – how to take fools for profit without changing hotels. So are you going to stop there?' Her head wagged in a firm negative. 'Huh-uh. The grift's like everything else. You don't stand still. You either go up or down, usually down, but my Roy's going up.'

Roy was guiltily flattered. He pointed out that however it was, it was still the con. It didn't have the dangers that the organized rackets had.

'It doesn't, huh?' Lilly asked. 'Well, you could have fooled me. Now, I heard of a guy just about your age who got hit so hard in the guts that it almost killed him.'

'Well, uh – '

'Sure, sure, that doesn't count. That's different. And

here's something else that's different.' She held up the burned hand. 'Do you know how I really got that burn? Well, I'll tell you . . .'

She told him, and he listened sickishly; shamed and embarrassed. Unwilling to associate such things with his mother, and unable to connect them with himself. Insofar as he could, they tended to widen the rift that lay between him and Lilly.

She saw how he felt; saw that it was no use. A slow fury welled through her tired body.

'So that's that,' she said, 'and it doesn't have anything to do with you, does it? Just another chapter in the Perils of Lilly Dillon.'

'And very interesting, too,' he said, his voice light. 'Maybe you should write a book, Lilly.'

'Maybe you should write one,' Lilly said. 'Carol Roberg would make a good chapter.'

Roy came stiffly to his feet. He nodded coldly, picked up his hat and started toward the door; then paused with a gesture of appeal. 'Lilly,' he said, 'just what are you driving at, anyway? What more can I do about Carol than I've already done?'

'You're asking me,' Lilly said bitterly. 'You've actually got the guts to stand there and ask me what you should do!'

'But – you're suggesting that I should marry her? Ask her to marry me? Oh, now, come off of it! What kind of break would that be for her?'

'Oh, God! God, God, God,' Lilly moaned.

Coloring, Roy slammed on his hat. 'I'm sorry I'm such a big disappointment to you. I'm going now.'

Lilly looked at him, as he still hesitated, and remarked that she hadn't noticed. 'That's the second time you've fooled me tonight,' she said. 'Now you see him and now you see him, and when he goes nobody knows.'

He left abruptly.

Striding down the corridor, his steps slowed and he paused; teetered on the point of turning back. At about the same instant, Lilly jumped up from her chair, started toward the door, and herself paused in teetering indecision.

They were so much alike, so much a part of one another. They were that close – for a moment.

The moment passed; a moment before murder. Then, flouting instinct, each made his decision. Each, as he always had, went his own way.

15

Roy had his delayed dinner in a downtown restaurant. He ate hungrily, telling himself, and doubtless meaning it, that it was good to be eating in a restaurant. It was what he was used to. The subtle sameness of the food, whatever the restaurant, had a reassuring quality about it, not unlike a mother's milk to a child. In its familiar and dependable nurture, it bolstered one's believe-or-perish credo that the more things changed the more they remained the same.

Similarly, it was good to be back in his own hotel bed. For here also would be his own bed wherever it was; standardized, always ready and waiting for him, simultaneously providing the pleasurable perquisites of permanence and impermanence. Perhaps, in his dreams, Carol briefly shared the bed with him, and he winced, almost crying out. But there were entirely amenable wraiths, also comfortably standardized, who came quickly to the rescue. They asked no more of him than he did of them, a sensual but immaculate penetration which achieved its end without mental or moral involvement. One bathed quickly or lingeringly, sans the danger of nearing the water.

So, all in all, Roy Dillon slept well that night.

Awakening early, he lay for a while in the presumable posture of all men awakening. Hands locked under his head, eyes gazing absently at the ceiling, letting his mind roam. Then, with a brisk abandonment of bed, he washed, dressed, and left the hotel.

He ate breakfast. He visited a barber shop, indulged himself in 'the works' and went back to his two-room suite. After bathing, he put on completely fresh clothes, hat and shoes included, and again left the hotel.

He got his car from its parking lot, and turned it out into the traffic.

At first he felt a little awkward, nervous, after his prolonged absence from driving. But that passed quickly. In a few blocks he was himself again, moving the car along with automatic ease, driving with the same unthinking skill that a stenographer applies to a typewriter. He was part of this river of cars, aiding its sluggish tide and in turn aided by it. Without losing his identity, free to turn out of the tide when he chose, he still belonged to something.

Like many business establishments that had once been a traditional integrand of the downtown's whole, the jobbing house of Sarber & Webb was now set down in a quasi-residential district; commodiously released, for a restless hiatus, from the sprawling giant which would inevitably surround it again. The firm was housed in a roomy sand-stone-and-brick building, a lofty one-story high for perhaps three-fourths of its area. At the rear it jutted up to a story-and-a-half, thus accommodating the company offices.

Roy put his car on the private lot at the side of the building. Whistling absently, his eyes approving as he surveyed the familiar scene around him, he took his briefcase from the car.

Someone else was looking them over too, he saw, but without his own casualness. A young man – well, perhaps he wasn't quite so young – in shirtsleeves but wearing a vest. A clerk in appearance, he stood well back on the wide sidewalk bordering the building, looking critically up and down and around, and occasionally jotting into a small notebook.

He turned and watched as Roy approached, his gaze uncompromising at first, incipiently disapproving. Then, as Roy came on, unflinching, and grinned and nodded, 'Hi,' the gaze registered a little warmth, and its proprietor nodded in return.

'Hi,' he said, almost as though the word embarrassed him.

Roy passed on, grinning, mentally shaking his head.

A long, broad service counter stretched along the interior front of the building, breached at one end by a wicket. Behind it, racks of stock-shelves ranged rearward, bulging neatly with the thousand-odd items which were wholesaled by Sarber & Webb, and forming a half-dozen parallel aisles.

It was early, and he was the only salesman-customer in the place. Usually at this hour, most of the clerks were either having coffee across the street or propped up along the counter in clusters, smoking and talking until they could resign themselves to the day. But there was no such homey nonsense this morning.

Everyone was present, without a cigarette or coffee carton in sight. The aisles hummed with activity: the pulling of orders, inventorying, restocking, dusting, and rearranging. Everyone was busy, or – much harder – pretending to be busy.

Through the years, he had become friendly with all of

them, and all came forward for a handshake and a word of congratulation on his recovery. But they wasted no time about it. Puzzled, Roy turned to the clerk who was opening a catalogue for him.

'What's hit this place?' he asked. 'I haven't seen anyone as busy since the joint caught fire.'

'Kaggs hit it, that's what!'

'Kaggs? Is that anything like the galloping crud?'

The clerk laughed grimly. 'You can say that again! Brother,' he brushed imaginary sweat from his brow. 'If that son-of-a-bitch stays around much longer – !'

Kaggs, he elaborated, was one of the home-office big shots, a seeming mixture of comptroller, troubleshooter, and efficiency expert. 'Came out here right after you went into the hospital – one of those college punks, he looks like. And he ain't had a kind word for anyone. Ain't no one knows anything but him, and everyone's either a dope-off or a bum. Now, you know that's not so, Roy. You won't find a harder-workin', more efficient group of boys anywhere than we got right here!'

'That's right,' Roy nodded agreeably, although it was very far from right. 'Maybe he'll run me off, d'you suppose?'

'I was going to tell you. He *did* chop off several of the salesmen; just won't wholesale to 'em any more. And what kind of sense does that make? They're all selling on commission. If they don't sell, they don't make nothing, so – *psst*, here he comes!'

As Roy had suspected, Kaggs was the critical-looking young man he had seen outside the building. A split second after the clerk had spoken, he was upon them, shooting out his hand like a weapon.

'Kaggs. Home office,' he said. 'Glad to meet you.'

'This is Mr Dillon,' the clerk said, nervously obsequious. 'Roy's one of our best salesmen, Mr Kaggs.'

'He is the best.' Kaggs didn't give the clerk a glance. 'Which isn't saying much for this place. Want to talk to you, Dillon.'

He turned, still clinging to Roy's hand as though to hustle him along. Roy remained where he was, pulling Kaggs back around with a jerk. He smiled pleasantly, as the home-office man blinked at him, startled.

'That was a pretty backhanded compliment, Mr Kaggs,' he said, 'and I never let people get away with things like that. If I did, I wouldn't be a good salesman.'

Kaggs considered the statement; nodded with curt judiciousness. 'You're right. I apologize. Now, I'd still like to talk to you.'

'Lead the way,' Roy said, picking up his briefcase.

Kaggs led him back down the counter, abruptly swerving away from the wicket and moving toward the building entrance. 'How about some coffee, okay? Sets a bad example; too much piddling around here already. But it's hard to talk with so many people trying to listen in.'

'You don't seem to think much of them,' Roy remarked.

Kaggs said crisply, as they started across the street, that he had no feelings at all about people in the abstract. 'It depends on how they stack up. If they're on the ball, I've got plenty of consideration for 'em.'

In the restaurant, he asked for milk as well as coffee, mixing the two together a little at a time as he sipped from his cup. 'Ulcers,' he explained. 'Your trouble too, right?' Then, without waiting for an answer he went on:

'Had you spotted when you passed me this morning, Dillon. Nothing slobby or sloppy about you. Looked like you were going somewhere and you knew the way. Figured then that you must be Dillon; connected you with your sales right away. And when I said that it didn't say much for Webb & Sarber – your being the best man, I mean – I meant just that. You stack up as a top-flight man in my book, but you've had no incentive here. No one walking on your heels. Just a lot of half-asses, so the tendency's been not to stretch yourself. I'm bouncing the slobs, incidentally. Makes no difference to me if they are only on commission. If they're not making good money, they're not giving us good representation and we can't afford to have 'em around. What's your selling experience, anyway? Before you came here, I mean?'

'Selling's all I've done since I left high school,' Roy said, not knowing what all this was leading up to but willing to go along for the ride. 'You name it, I've sold it. All door-to-door stuff. Premiums, brushes, pots and pans, magazines.'

'You're singing my song,' Kaggs grinned crookedly. 'I'm the guy who worked his way through college peddling subscriptions. You switched to business-house selling when you came with us; why?'

'It's easier to get into doors,' Roy said, 'and you can build up regular customers. The house-to-house stuff is mostly one-shot.'

Kaggs nodded approvingly. 'Ever supervise salesmen? You know; kind of head them up, keep 'em on their toes.'

'I've run house-to-house crews,' Roy shrugged. 'Who hasn't?'

'I haven't. Don't have the talent for it, somehow.'

'Or tact?' Roy smiled.

'Or tact. But never mind me; I do all right. The point is, Webb & Sarber need a sales manager. Should have had one right along. Someone who's proved he's a salesman and can handle other salesmen. He'd have a lot of deadwood to clear out, or put some sap back into 'em. Hire new men, and give 'em a good draw if they cut the stuff. What do you think?'

'I think it's a good idea,' Roy said.

'Now, I don't know offhand what your best year's earnings have been. Around sixty-six hundred, I believe. But put it this way. We'll top your best year by fifteen hundred; make it eight thousand in round numbers. That's just a beginning, of course. Give you a year at eight, and if you're not worth a lot more than that by then I'll kick you the hell out. But I know you will be worth more. Knew you were my kind of man from the minute I saw you this morning. And now that we've got that settled, I'm going to borrow one of your cigarettes and have a real cup of coffee, and if my stomach doesn't like it I'll kick it the hell out, too.'

Roy held out his cigarette package. In the rapid-fire delivery of Kaggs talk, he had let its meaning slip away from him. And coming to him abruptly, hitting him like a blow, his hand gave a convulsive jerk.

Kaggs looked at him, blinking. 'Something wrong? Incidentally, don't cigarettes and coffee bother you? Your ulcers, I mean.'

Roy nodded, shook his head. 'I, uh, it wasn't a bad ulcer. Just happened to be in a bad place. Struck a vein. I – look, Mr Kaggs – '

'Perk, Roy. Perk for Percy, and smile when you say that. How old are you, Roy? Twenty-five or -six? Fine. No reason at all why you can't . . .'

Roy's mind raced desperately. A *sales manager!* Him, Roy

Dillon, grifter de luxe, a sales manager! But he couldn't be, damnit! It would be too confining, too proscribed. He would lose the freedom of movement necessary to carrying on the grift. The job itself, the importance of it, would preclude any such activities. As a commission salesman, he might reasonably loiter in the places where the grift could be practiced. But as Webb & Sarber's sales manager – no! The slightest rumble would dump him cold.

He couldn't take the job. On the other hand, how could he turn it down, without arousing suspicion? How could you reasonably refuse a job that was right up your alley, one that was not only much better than the one you had but promised to become far, far better?

'. . . glad to get this thing settled, Roy,' Perk Kaggs was saying. 'Now, we've wasted enough time here, so if you're through with your coffee – '

'Mr Kaggs – Perk,' Roy said. 'I can't take the job. I can't take it right away, I mean. This is the first day I've been up and around, and I just dropped by to say hello and – '

'Oh?' Kaggs looked at him judiciously. 'Well, you do look a little pale. How soon will you be ready, a week?'

'Well, I – the doctor's checking me over in a week, but I'm not sure that – '

'Two weeks then. Or take a little longer if you have to. Be plenty of work, and you've got to be in shape for it.'

'But you need a man right now! It wouldn't be fair to you to – '

'I take care of the being-fair-to-me department.' Kaggs permitted himself an icy grin. 'Things been going to hell this long. They can go a little longer.'

'But – '

But there was nothing more to say. Perhaps he could think of an out for himself during the next week or so, but none occurred to him now.

They walked back across the street together, and then he went on by himself to his car. He got into it uncertainly, started the motor, then cut it off again.

What now? How could he pass the time that Kaggs had given him? Selling was out of the question, of course, since he was supposedly unready to work. But there was the other, his real occupation; the source of the wealth behind the four clown pictures.

He started the car again. Then, with a dismayed grunt, he again shut it off. Since work was out, so also was the grift. He wouldn't dare turn a trick. Not before the week-end, at least, when he would normally be idle and could unsuspiciously indulge in some on-the-towning.

The weekend. And this was only Wednesday.

He thought about Moira. With an unconscious frown, he dismissed her from his mind. Not today. It was too soon after Carol.

Starting his car for the third time, he drove around for a couple of hours, then had lunch at a drive-in and returned to the hotel. He spent a restless afternoon reading. He had dinner, and killed the evening at the movies.

Faced with more idleness the following day, he was again moved to call Moira. But somehow, without seeming to think about it, he rang Carol's number instead.

Coming to the phone drowsy-voiced, she said she could not see him. They had no reason to see each other.

'Oh, now, we might have,' he said. 'Why don't we get together and talk about it?'

She hesitated. 'About what, exactly?'

'Well . . . you know. A lot of things. We'll have lunch, and – '

'No,' she said firmly. 'No, Roy. It is impossible, anyway. I am working regularly at the hospital now. Night duty. In the day, I must sleep.'

'In the evening, then.' Suddenly it had become very important that he see her. 'Before you go to work. Or I can pick you up in the morning, after you finish. I . . .'

He rushed on. He had a new job, he explained. Or, well, he was *thinking* about taking a new job. He wanted her opinion on it, and –

'No,' she said. 'No, Roy.'

And she hung up.

16

On the following day, he called Moira Langtry. But there again he was defeated. He was surprised as well as irritated, since, momentarily, she had seemed to welcome an early start on their La Jolla weekend, reversing herself in practically the same breath. It couldn't be done, she explained. At least, due to delicate womanly reasons, a periodic difficulty, it wouldn't be very practical. Tomorrow? Mmm, no, she was afraid not. But the next day, Sunday, should be fine.

Roy suspected that she was simply a little miffed at him; that this was his punishment for his weeks of inattentiveness. Certainly, however, he was of no mind to plead with her, so he said casually that Sunday would be fine with him, too, and the arrangements were made on that basis.

He killed the rest of that day, or most of it, with a trip to the Santa Monica beaches. The next day being Saturday, he was free to hit the grift again. But after some mental shilly-shallying, he decided against it.

Let it go. He wasn't quite in the mood. He needed to snap out of himself a little more, to shake off certain disturbing memories which might add to the hazards of a profession which already had hazards enough.

He loafed through the day, he became broody; almost, he pitied himself. What a way to live, he thought resentfully. Always watching every word he said, carefully scrutinizing every word that was said to him. And never making a move that wasn't studiously examined in advance. Figuratively, he walked through life on a high wire, and he could turn his mind from it only at his own peril.

Of course, he was well-paid for his efforts. The loot had piled up fast, and it would go on piling up. But there was the trouble – it simply piled up! As useless to him as so many soap coupons.

Needless to say, this state of things would not go on forever; he would not forever live a second-class life in a second-class hotel. In another five years, his grifted loot would total enough for retirement, and he could drop caution with the grift which impelled it. But those five years were necessary to insure that retirement, filling it with all the things he had been forced to forego. And just suppose he didn't live five years. Or even one year. Or even one day. Or –

The brooding exhausted itself. And him, as well. The interminable day passed, and he fell asleep. And then, wondrously, it was morning. Then, at last, he had something to do.

They were making the trip by train, the southbound one-o'clock, and Moira was meeting him at the station. Roy parked his car on the railroad lot – he would rent another for their holiday use – and took his bag out of the trunk.

It was only a quarter after twelve, far too early to expect Moira. Roy bought their tickets, gave the seat numbers and his bag to a well-tipped redcap, and entered the station bar.

He had a drink, stretching it out as he glanced occasionally at the clock. At twenty minutes to one, he got up from his stool and went back through the entrance.

The Sunday southbound was always crowded, carrying not only the civilian traffic but the swarms of Marines and sailors returning to their duty stations at Camp Pendleton and San Diego. Roy watched as they streamed through the numbered gates and down the long ramps which led to the trains. A little nervously, he again checked the time.

Ten minutes until one. That was enough time, of course, but not too much. The station was more than a block in depth, and the train ramp was practically a block long. If Moira didn't get here very quickly, she might as well stay home.

Five minutes until one.

Four minutes.

Sourly, Roy gave up and started back to the bar. She wouldn't do this deliberately, he was sure. Probably, she'd been caught up in a traffic jam, one of the Gordian-knots of snarled-up cars which afflicted the city's supposedly highspeed freeways. But, damnit, if she'd ever start any place a little early, instead of waiting until the last minute – !

He heard his name called.

He whirled and saw her coming through the entrance, trotting behind the redcap who carried her baggage. The man flashed a smile at Roy as he passed. 'Do my best, boss. Just you stay behind me.'

Roy grabbed Moira and hurried her along with him.

'Sorry,' she panted. 'Darned apartment house! Elevator stuck, an' – '

'Never mind. Save your breath,' he said.

They raced the marble-floored length of the building, passed through the gate and on down into the seemingly endless stretch of ramp. At its far end a trainman stood, watch in hand. As they approached, he pocketed the watch, and started up the short side-ramp to the loading platform.

They followed him, passed him.

As the train pulled out, they caught the last car.

A train porter escorted them to their seats. Breathless, they slumped into them. And for the next thirty minutes, they hardly stirred.

At last, as they were pulling out of the town of Fullerton, Moira's head turned on the white-slipped seat back and she grinned at him.

'You're a good man, McGee.'

'And you're a good woman, Mrs Murphy,' he said. 'What's your secret?'

'Underwear in the chowder, natch. What's yours?'

Roy said his derived from inspirational reading. 'I was reading a wonderful story just as you came in. Author named Bluegum LaBloat. Ever hear of him?'

'Mmm, it does sound slightly familiar.'

'I think this is the best thing he's done,' Roy said. 'The setting is the men's washroom in a bus station, and the characters are a clean old man and a fat young boy who live in one of the coin toilets. They ask little of the world. Only the privacy incident to doing what comes naturally. But do they get it? Heck, no! Every time they begin to function – you should excuse the language – some diarrheal dope rushes up and drops a dime in the slot. And in his coarse surrender to need, their own desire is lost. In the end, fruition frustrated, they gather up the apple cores from the urinals and go off into the woods to bake a pie.'

Moira gave him a severe look.

'I'm going to call the conductor,' she declared.

'I couldn't buy your silence with a drink?'

'The silence I'll buy – a couple of hours of it, after that. You buy the drink, and be sure you rinse your mouth out with it.'

Roy laughed. 'I'll wait for you if you like.'

'Go,' Moira said firmly, closing her eyes and leaning back against the seat. 'Go, boy, go!'

Roy patted her on the flank. Rising, he walked the two cars to the bar-lounge. He was feeling good again, back in form. The brooding introspectiveness of recent days had slipped from him, and he felt like swinging.

As he had expected, the lounge was crowded. Unless he could squeeze in with some group, which was what he intended to do, there was no place to sit.

He surveyed the scene approvingly, then turned to the attendant behind the small bar. 'I'll have a bourbon and water,' he said. 'Bonded.'

'Sorry, sir. Can't serve you unless you're seated.'

'Let's see. How much is it, anyway?'

'Eighty-five cents, sir. But I can't – '

'Two dollars,' Roy nodded, laying two bills on the counter. 'Exact change, right?'

He got his drink. Glass in hand, he started down the aisle, swaying occasionally with the movement of the train. Halfway down the car, he allowed himself to be swayed against a booth where four servicemen sat, jolting their drinks and slopping a little of his own on the table.

He apologized profusely. 'You've got to let me buy you a round. No, I insist. Waiter!'

Vastly pleased, they urged him to sit down, squeezing over in the booth to make room. The drinks came, and disappeared. Over their protests, he bought another round.

'But it ain't fair, pal. We're buyin' the next time.'

'No sweat,' Roy said pleasantly. 'I'm not sure I can drink another one, but . . .'

He broke off, glancing down at the floor. He frowned, squinted. Then, stooping, he reached slightly under the booth. And straightening again, he dropped a small dotted cube on the table.

'Did one of you fellows drop this?' he asked.

The tat rolled. The bets doubled and redoubled. With the deceptive swiftness of the train, the money streamed into Roy Dillon's pockets. When his four dupes thought about him later, it would be as a 'helluva nice guy,' so amiably troubled by his unwanted and unintended winnings as to make shameful any troubled thought of their own. When Roy thought about them later – but he would not. All his thinking was concentrated on *them*, the time of their fleecing; in keeping them constantly diverted and disarmed. And in the high intensity of that concentration, in fueling its white-hot flames, he had nothing of them left for afterthoughts. They enjoyed their drinks; his were tasteless. Occasionally, one of them went to the toilet; he could not. Now and then, they looked out the window, remarking on the beauty of the passing scenery – for it was beautiful with the snowy beaches, the green and gold of the groves, the blue-gray mountains and the white houses with red-tiled roofs: strikingly reminiscent of the South of France. But while Roy chimed in with appropriate comments, he did not look where they looked nor see what they saw. At last, swarming up out of his concentration, he saw that the car had emptied and that the train was creeping through the industrial outskirts of San Diego, the terminus of the rail trip. Rising, wringing hands all around with the servicemen, he turned to leave the bar-lounge. And there was Moira smiling at him from its head.

'Thought I'd better come looking for you,' she said. 'Have fun?'

'Oh, you know. Just rolling for drinks,' he shrugged. 'Sorry I left you alone so long.'

'Forget it,' she smiled, taking his arm. 'I didn't mind a bit.'

17

R oy rented a car at San Diego, and they drove out to
their La Jolla hotel. It sat in a deep lawn, high on a
bluff overlooking the Pacific. Moira was delighted
with it. Breathing in the clean cool air, she insisted on a
brief tour of the grounds before they went inside.

'Now, this is something like,' she declared. 'This is living!'
And sliding a sultry glance at him. 'I don't know how I'll
show my appreciation.'

'Oh, I'll think of something,' Roy said. 'Maybe you can
rinse out my socks for me.'

He registered for them, and they followed the bellboy
upstairs. Their rooms were on opposite sides of a corridor,
and Moira looked at him quizzically, demanding an
explanation.

'Why the apartheid bit?' she said. 'Not that I can't stand
it, if you can.'

'I thought it would be better that way, separate rooms
under our own names. Just in case there's any trouble, you
know.'

'Why should there be any trouble?'

Roy said easily that there shouldn't be any; there was no
reason why there should be. 'But why take chances? After

all, we're right across from each other. Now, if you'd like me to show you how convenient it is . . .'

He pulled her into his arms, and they stood locked together for a moment. But when he started to take it from there, she pulled away.

'Later, hmm?' She stooped before the mirror, idly prinking at her hair. 'I hurried so fast this morning that I'm only half-thrown together.'

'Later it is,' Roy nodded agreeably. 'Like something to eat now, or would you rather wait for dinner?'

'Oh, dinner by all means. I'll give you a ring.'

He left her, still stooped before the mirror, and crossed to his own room. Unpacking his bag, he decided that she was curious rather than peeved about the separate rooms, and that, in any case, the arrangement was imperative. He was known as a single man. Departing from that singleness, he would have to use an assumed name. And where then was his protective front, so carefully and painfully built up through the years?

He was bound to the front, bound to and bound by it. If Moira was puzzled or peeved, then she could simply get over being puzzled or peeved. He wished he hadn't had to explain to her, since explanations were always bad. He also regretted that she had seen him operating in the club car. But the wish and the regret were small things, idly reflective rather than worrisome.

Anyone might do a little gambling for drinks. Anyone might be cautious about hotel registrations. Why should Moira regard the first as a professional activity, and the second as a cover for it – a front which must always accrue to him like a shadow?

Unpacked, Roy stretched out on the bed, surprisingly grateful for the chance to rest. He had not realized that he was so tired, that he could be so glad to lie down. Apparently, he reflected, he was still not fully recovered from the effects of his hemorrhage.

Lulled by the distant throb of the ocean, he fell into a comfortable doze, awakening just before dusk. He stretched lazily and sat up, unconsciously smiling with the pleasure of his comfort. Salt-scented air wafted in through the windows. Far off to the West, beneath a pastel sky, an orange-red sun sank slowly into the ocean. Many times he had seen the sun set off the Southern California coast, but each time was a new experience. Each sunset seemed more beautiful than the last.

Reluctantly, as the phone rang, he turned away from its splendor. Moira's voice came gaily over the wire.

'Boo, you ugly man! Are you buying me dinner or not?'

'Absolutely not,' he said. 'Give me one good reason why I should.'

'Can't. Not over the phone.'

'Write me a letter, then.'

'Can't. No mail deliveries on Sunday.'

'Excuses,' he grumbled. 'Always excuses! Well, okay, but it's strictly hamburgers.'

They had cocktails on the hotel's patio bar. Then, driving farther on in to the city, they ate at a seafood restaurant jutting out over the ocean. Moira had declared an armistice with her diet, and she proved that she meant it.

The meal opened with a lobster cocktail, practically a meal in itself. Served with hot garlic-bread and a fresh green salad, the main course was a sizzling platter of assorted seafoods bordered by a rim of delicately-browned potatoes. Then came dessert – a fluffy cheesecake – and pots of black, black coffee.

Moira sighed happily as she accepted a cigarette. 'As I said earlier, this is living! I honestly don't think I can move!'

'Then, of course you don't feel like dancing.'

'Silly,' she said. 'Whatever gave you an idea like that?'

She loved dancing, and she danced very well; as, for that matter, did he. More than once, he caught the eyes of other patrons on them; seeing them also, Moira pressed closer to him, bending her supple body to his.

After perhaps an hour of dancing, when the floor became oppressively crowded, they went for a moonlight drive up the coast, turning around and heading back at the city of Oceanside. The mounting waves of the night tide foamed with phosphorus. They came rolling in from the distant depths of the ocean, striking against the shore in a steady series of thunder-like roars. On the rocky outcrops of the shore, an occasional seal gleamed blackly.

It was almost eleven when Roy got them back to their hotel, and Moira was suppressing a yawn. She apologized, saying it was the weather, not the company. But when they again stood in front of their rooms, she held out her hand in good night.

'You don't mind, do you, Roy? It's been such a wonderful evening, I guess I just wore myself out.'

'Of course you did,' he said. 'I'm pretty tired myself.'

'You're sure now? You're sure you don't mind?'

'Beat it,' he said, pushing her through her door. 'It's okay.'

But of course it wasn't okay, and he minded a great deal. He entered his own room, restraining an angry urge to slam the door. Stripping out of his clothes, he sat down on the edge of the bed; puffed surlily at a cigarette. A hell of a holiday, this was! It would serve her right if he walked out on her!

The phone tinkled faintly. It was Moira. She spoke with repressed laughter.

'Open your door.'

'What?' He grinned expectantly. 'What for?'

'Open it and find out, you fathead!'

He hung up and opened his door. There was a sibilant, '*Gangway!*' from the door opposite his. And he stood back. And Moira came skipping across the hall. Her black hair stood in a sedate pile on her head. She was completely naked. Gravely, a finger under her chin, she curtsied before him.

'I hope you don't mind, sir,' she said. 'I just washed my clothes, and I couldn't do a thing with them.'

Then, gurgling, choking with laughter, she collapsed in his arms. 'Oh, you!' she gasped. 'If you could have seen your face when I told you good night! You looked s-so – so – *ah, ha, ha –*'

He picked her up and tossed her on the bed.

They had a hell of a time.

18

B ut afterward, after she had gone back to her own room, depression came to him and what had seemed like such a hell of a time became distasteful, even a little disgusting. It was the depression of surfeit, the tail of self-indulgence's kite. You flew high, wide, and handsome, imposing on the breeze that might have wafted you along indefinitely; and then it was gone, and down, down, down you went.

Tossing restlessly in the darkness, Roy told himself that the gloom was natural enough and a small enough price to pay for what he had received. But as to the last, at least, he was not convinced. There was too much of a sameness about the evening's delights. He had been the same route too many times. He'd been there before, so double-damned often, and however you traveled – backward, forward, or walking on your hands – you always got to the same place. You got nowhere, in other words, and each trip took a little more out of you.

Still, did he really want anything changed? Even now, in his misery, weren't his thoughts already reaching out and across the hall?

He flung his legs over the side of the bed, and sat up.

Lighting a cigarette, pulling a robe around his shoulders, he sat looking out into the moonlit night. Thinking that perhaps it wasn't him or them – he or Moira – that had brought him to this gloomy despair. Perhaps it was a combination of things.

He didn't have his strength back yet. He'd used up a lot of energy in catching the train. And grifting after so long an idleness had been unusually straining on him. Then there'd been a lot of little things – Moira's curiosity about the separate rooms, for example. And that heavy dinner, at least twice as much as he needed or wanted. Then, after all that . . .

His mind went back to the dinner now, the enormous quantity and richness of it. And suddenly the cigarette tasted lousy to him, and a wave of nausea surged up through his stomach. He ran to the bathroom, a hand over his mouth, cheeks bulging. And he got there barely in time.

He rid himself of the food, every miserable mouthful of it. He rinsed out his mouth with warm water, then drank several glasses of cold. And immediately he began vomiting again.

Bending over the sink, he anxiously studied his stomach's washings, and to his relief he found them clear. There was no tell-tale trace of brown that would signify internal bleeding.

Shivering a little, he tottered back to bed and pulled the covers over him. He felt a lot better now, lighter and cleaner. He closed his eyes, and was promptly asleep.

He slept soundlessly, dreamlessly; seeming to compress two hours of sleep in one. Awakening at about six-thirty, he knew he'd had his quota and that further sleep was out of the question.

He shaved, showered and dressed. That took no more than a half-hour, drag it out as he would. So there it was, only seven o'clock in the morning, and he as much at loose ends as if he was back in LA.

Certainly, he couldn't call Moira at such an hour. Moira had indicated last night that she intended to sleep until noon, and that she would cheerfully murder anyone who awakened her before then. At any rate, he was in no hurry at all to see Moira. It was labor enough to pull himself together again, without the necessity of entertaining her.

Going down to the hotel coffee shop, he had some toast and coffee. But he only did it as a matter of discipline, of virtue. Regardless of nights-before, a man ate breakfast in the morning. He ate, hungry or not, or else he inevitably found himself in trouble.

Strolling down a white-graveled walk to the cliff above the ocean, he let his eyes rove aimlessly over the expanse of sea and sand: The icy-looking whitecaps, the blinking, faraway sails of boats, the sweeping, constantly searching gulls. Desolation. Eternal, infinite. Like Dostoevski's conception of eternity, a fly circling about a privy, the few signs of life only emphasized the loneliness.

At this hour of the morning, a very little of it went a long way with Roy Dillon. Abruptly, he turned away from it and headed for the rented car.

The coffee and toast hadn't set at all well with him. He needed something to settle his stomach, and he could think of only one thing that would do it. A bottle of good beer, or, better still, ale. And he knew it was not to be found, so early in the day, in a community like La Jolla. The bars here, the cocktail lounges, rather, would not open until shortly before lunch. If there were morning drinkers in the town, and doubtless there were, they had their own private bars to drink from.

Turning the car toward San Diego, Roy drove out of the southerly outskirts of La Jolla and into the more humble districts beyond, slowing occasionally for a swift appraisal of the various drinking establishments. Many of them were open, but they were not the right kind. They would have only the West Coast beers, which, to Roy's way of thinking, were undrinkable. None of them, certainly, would have a good ale.

Nearing San Diego, he drove up Mission Valley for a mile or so; then, swinging up a long hill, he entered Mission Hills. There, after some thirty minutes of wandering about, he found what he was looking for. It wasn't a fancy place at all; not one of those glossy cocktail lounges where drinks were secondary to atmosphere. Just a good solid-looking bar, with an air that immediately inspired confidence.

The proprietor was counting cash into his register when Roy entered. A graying, wiry-looking man, with a tanned smile-wrinkled face, he nodded a greeting in the back-bar mirror. 'Yes, sir, what'll it be?'

Roy put a name to it, and the proprietor said that certainly he had good ale: if ale wasn't good it was slop. 'Give you imported or Ballantine's.' Roy chose Ballantine's, and the proprietor was pleased at his gratified reaction.

'Good, huh? Y'know, I think I'll just have one myself.'

Roy took an immediate liking to the guy, and the feeling was reciprocated. He liked the look of this place, its unassuming honesty and decency; the quiet pride of its owner in being its owner.

Within ten minutes they were on a first-name basis. Roy was explaining his presence in town, using his holidaying as an excuse for off-hour drinking. Bert – the proprietor – revealed that he also shunned the pre-noon drink; but he was going on vacation tomorrow, so what was the harm, anyway?

Two men came in, downed a double-shot each, and hurried out again. Bert looked after them with a touch of sadness, and came back to Roy. That was no way to drink, he said. Occasionally, even the best of men needed a drink or two in the morning, but they shouldn't drink it that way.

As he left to wait on another customer, he brushed against a back-bar display stand of salted nuts, moving it slightly out of its original position. And staring absently in that direction, Roy saw something that made him frown. He stood up a little from his stool for another look, making sure of what he had seen. He sat down again, puzzled and troubled.

A punchboard! A punchboard in a place like this! Bert was no fool, either in the con or the everyday sense, but a punchboard was strictly a fool's item.

Back at the time Roy was just starting out, there were still a few teams working the boards, one man planting them, the other knocking them over. But he hadn't seen any in years. Everyone had tipped long ago, and trying to plant a board now was the equivalent of asking for a busted jaw.

Of course, some small merchants and barkeeps still bought boards on their own, punching out the winning numbers at the start and thus giving the suckers no chance at all. But Bert wouldn't do that. Bert . . .

Roy laughed wryly to himself, took a foamy sip of the ale. What was this, anyway? Was he, Roy Dillon, actually concerned about the honesty or dishonesty of a barkeep or the possibility that he might be swindled?

Another customer had come in, a khaki-clad workman, and Bert was serving him a coke. Coming back down the bar with two fresh bottles of ale, he refilled their glasses. And Roy allowed himself to 'notice' the board.

'Oh, that thing.' The proprietor retrieved it from the back-bar and laid it in front of him. 'Some fellow walked out and left it here three or four months ago. Didn't notice it until after he was gone. I was going to throw it away, but I get a customer now and then who wants to try his luck. So . . .' He paused tentatively. 'Want to have a try? Chances run from a cent to a dollar.'

'Well . . .' Roy looked down at the board.

Affixed to the top were five gold-colored imitation coins, representing cash prizes of five to one hundred dollars. Under each of them a number was printed. To win, one had only to punch out a corresponding number or numbers from the thousands on the board.

None of the winners had been punched out. Bert, obviously, was as honest as he looked.

'Well,' said Roy, picking up the little metal key which dangled from the board, 'what can I lose?'

He punched a few numbers, laying them out for Bert's inspection. On his sixth punch, he hit the five-dollar prize, and the proprietor smilingly laid the money on the counter. Roy let it lay, again poised the key over the board.

He couldn't tell Bert that this was a chump's gimmick. To do so would reveal knowledge that no honest man should have. Most certainly, and even though someone else was bound to do it, he couldn't take the man himself. The grift just wasn't for him today – or so he rationalized. There just wasn't enough at stake.

If he knocked off every prize on the board, the take would be under two hundred dollars. And naturally he'd never get away with knocking them all off. The pros of the racket had always gone for the big one and left the others alone. He, however, had already hit the five, so . . .

He punched out the ten-dollar number. Still smiling, pleased rather than disconcerted, Bert again laid money on the counter. Roy brought the key up for another punch.

This was the way to do it, he'd decided. The way to get the board out of circulation. One more prize – the twenty-five – and he'd point out that something must be screwy about the board. Bert would be obliged to get rid of it. And he, of course, would refuse to accept his winnings.

He punched out the third 'lucky' number. Properly startled, he cleared his throat for the tip-off. But Bert, his smile slightly stiffened now, had turned to glance at the coke customer.

'Yes, sir?' he said. 'Something else?'

'Yes, sir,' the man said, his voice grimly light. 'Yes, sir, there's something else, all right. You got a federal gambling-tax stamp?'

'*Huh!* What – '

'Don't have one, huh? Well, I'll tell you something else you don't have; won't have it long, anyway. Your liquor license.'

'B-but – ' Bert had paled under his tan. California liquor licenses were worth a small fortune. 'B-but you can't do that! We were just – '

'Tell it to the state and Federal boys. I'm local.' He flipped open a leather credential-case; nodded coldly at Roy.

'You're pretty stupid, mister. No one but a stupe would knock a chump off for three balls in a row.'

Roy looked at him evenly. 'I don't know what you're talking about,' he said. 'And I don't like your language.'

'On your feet! I'm arresting you for bunco!'

'You're making a mistake, officer. I'm a salesman, and I – '

'You giving me a hard time? Huh? *Hah?* Why, you grifting son-of-a-bitch – !'

He grabbed Roy by the lapels, yanked him furiously to his feet and slammed him up against the wall.

19

First, there was the search; the turning out of pockets, the probing and slapping of garments, the hand brought up on either side of the testicles. Then came the questions, the demanded answers that were immediately labeled lies.

'*Your right name, goddamn you! Never mind them phony credentials! All you hustlers got 'em!*'

'That is my right name. I live in Los Angeles, and I've worked for the same company for four years – '

'*Stop lying! Who's working the boards with you? How many other places you pulled this gimmick?*'

'My health has been bad. I came down to La Jolla last night – a friend and I – on a holiday.'

'*All right, all right! Now, we're gonna start all over again and, by God, you better come clean!*'

'Officer, there are at least a hundred businessmen here in town who can identify me. I've been selling to them for years, and – '

'*Drop it! Drop that crap! Now, what's your right name!*'

The same questions over and over. The same answers over and over. Now and then, the cop turned to the wall telephone to pass his information on for checking. But still, the information checking out, he would not give up. He knew what he knew. With his own eyes, he had seen the bunco worked, a punchboard swiftly knocked for three prizes. And Roy's perfect front notwithstanding, how could the clear evidence of grifting be ignored?

He was on the phone again now, his heavy face sullen as he got the answers to his questions. Roy sidled a glance at the bar owner, Bert. He looked at the punchboard on the counter fixedly, and again raised his eyes to Bert. Nodded to him ever so slightly. But he couldn't be sure that Bert got the message.

The cop slammed up the phone. He stared at Roy sourly, rubbed a meaty hand over his face. Hesitating, he tried to form the words which the situation called for, the apology which outraged instinct and flouted the evidence of his own eyes.

From up the bar, Roy heard a dull grinding sound, the garbage disposal.

He grinned quietly to himself. 'Well, officer,' he said. 'Any more questions?'

'That's all.' The cop jerked his head. 'Looks like I maybe made a mistake.'

'Yes? You slam me around and insult me, and treat me like a criminal. And then you say you maybe made a mistake. That's supposed to smooth everything over.'

'Well –' mouth tight, choking over the words. 'Sorry. 'Pologize. No offence.'

Roy was content to settle for that. Savagely, the cop turned on Bert.

'All right, mister! I want the number of your liquor license! I'm turning you in for – for – *Where's that punchboard?*

'What punchboard?'

'Damn you, don't you pull that crap on me! The board that was right there on the counter – the one that this guy was playing! Now, you either hand it over or I'll find it myself!'

Bert picked up a rag, and began mopping the counter. 'I usually clean up this time of day,' he said. 'Clear up all the odds and ends of junk, and throw 'em down the garbage disposer. Now, I can't say that I remember any punchboard, but if there was one here . . .'

'You threw it away! Y-you think you can get away with that?'

'Can't I?' Bert said.

The cop stammered in furious incoherence. He said, 'You'll see, by God, you'll see!' And turning savagely to Roy, 'You too, mister! You ain't got me fooled a damned bit! I'm gonna be on the lookout for you, and the next time you hit this town – !'

He whirled and stalked out of the place. Grinning, Roy sat back down at his stool.

'Acts like he's sore about something,' he said. 'How about another ale?'

'No,' Bert said.

'What? Now, look, Bert. I'm sorry if there was any trouble, but it was your punchboard. I didn't – '

'I know. It was my mistake. But I never make the same mistake twice. Now, I want you to leave and I don't want you to come back.'

Another customer came in, and Bert began to wait on him. Roy arose and walked out.

The dazzling sunlight struck against his face, its strength doubled with the contrast of the cool and shadowed bar.

The cold ale – how much had he drunk, anyway? – roiled in his stomach, then uneasily settled back. He wasn't drunk, by any means. He never got drunk. But it wasn't smart to start back to La Jolla without eating.

There was a small restaurant around the next corner, and he had a bowl of soup there and two cups of black coffee. Startled, he noticed the time as he left, five minutes after one, and he glanced around for a telephone. But the place apparently had none; no public phone, at any rate, so he went on out to his car.

It was probably best not to call Moira, he decided. The police would have called her, and he didn't want to make explanations over the phone.

He went back down the long hill to Mission Valley, then took the road left toward the coast. It was about twenty minutes' drive to La Jolla, twenty-five minutes at the outside. Then, he would be back at the hotel with Moira, lightly explaining the cop trouble as a –

A case of mistaken identity? No, no. Something more ordinary, something that might logically evolve from an innocent circumstance. This car, for example, was a rented car. The last driver might have been involved in a serious traffic violation; he had fled, say, from the scene of an accident. So when the police spotted the car this morning . . .

Well, sure, there were inconsistencies in the story: the police would have known it was a rented car by the license number. But that wasn't up to him to explain. He'd been the victim of a police booboo; who could figure out their mistakes?

A hell of a morning, he thought. It was Bert's punchboard. Why should he get tough with me? What the hell do I care what a barkeep thinks?

Near the intersection with Pacific Highway, the traffic about him thickened, and at the Highway itself it was stalled in a four-lane tangle which two cops were struggling to undo. That didn't jibe with the normal pattern of Monday in San Diego. Traffic wasn't this bad even during the shift-changes at the aircraft plants, and it was the wrong hour for that.

The cars crept forward slowly, Roy's car moving with them. Almost an hour later, near Mission Beach, he turned off the highway and into a filling station. And here he learned the reason for the congestion.

The horses were running at Del Mar. It was the beginning of the local racing season.

In another thirty minutes, the traffic had thinned, and rejoining it, he reached La Jolla some twenty minutes later. So he was very late, and entering the hotel he called Moira's room from the lobby. There was no answer, but she had left a message for him with the clerk.

'Why, yes, Mr Dillon. She said to tell you she'd gone to the races.'

'The races?' Roy frowned. 'You're sure?'

'Yes, sir. But she was only going to stay for part of the day's program. She'll be back early, she said.'

'I see,' Roy nodded. 'By the way, was there a call from the police about me a couple of hours ago?'

The clerk admitted delicately that there had been, also revealing that there had been a similar call to Mrs Langtry. 'Naturally, we spoke of you in the highest terms, Mr Dillon. It was, uh, nothing serious, I hope?'

'Nothing, thanks,' Roy said, and he went on up to his room.

He stood for some time before the French windows,

staring out at the sun-sparkled sea. Then, eyes hurting a little, he stretched out on the bed, letting his thoughts roam at will; piecing them together with hunch and instinct until they formed a pattern.

First there was her curiosity about the way he lived, the job he held. Why did he stay on, year after year, at a place like the Grosvenor-Carlton? Why did he cling, year after year, to a relatively small-time commission job? Then, there were her subtle complaints about their relationship: they didn't really *know* each other; they needed to 'get acquainted.' So he had arranged this excursion, a means of getting acquainted, and how did she use the time? Why, by putting him on his own, at every opportunity. And then sitting back to see what happened.

So now she knew; she must know. Her actions today proved that she did.

The police had called her about him, yet she had not been concerned. She had known that he would be all right, that just as his front had held up for years, it would continue to hold up in this trouble, whatever that trouble was. So, having found out all that she needed to, she had gone off to the races.

The races . . .

Abruptly, he sat up scowling, his mild annoyance with her turning to anger.

She had stalled on coming to La Jolla. After being so anxious for the trip, she had unreasonably found reason to postpone it – until this week.

Because this was the beginning of the Del Mar meet. And the tracks in the LA area were temporarily inactive.

Or . . . maybe not. He couldn't be absolutely sure that she was nosing into Lilly's business as she had nosed into his. It might be that she was simply sore at him for leaving her alone so long, and that she had gone to the races as a way of expressing her displeasure.

Moira returned to the hotel around four o'clock. Fretting humorously over the discomforts of her cab ride; pretending to pout at Roy for going off without her.

'I just thought I'd teach you a lesson, you big stinker! You're not mad, are you?'

'I'm not sure. I understand that the police called you about me.'

'Oh, that,' she shrugged. 'What was the trouble, anyway?'

'You wouldn't have any idea?'

'Well . . .' She began to draw in a little bit. Coming over to the bed, she sat down gingerly at his side. 'Roy, I've been wanting to talk to you for a long time. But before I could, I wanted to make sure that – '

'Let it ride a little,' he said carelessly. 'Did you see Lilly at the races?'

'Lilly? Oh, you mean your mother. Isn't she living in Los Angeles now?'

Roy said that she was. 'But the LA meets closed last week. So she'd be down here at Del Mar, wouldn't she?'

'How do I know? What are you getting at, anyway?'

She started to get up. He held her, taking a grip on the front of her dress.

'Now, I'll ask you again. Did you see Lilly at the Del Mar track?'

'No! How could I? I sat in the clubhouse!'

Roy smiled thinly, pointing out her blunder. 'And Lilly wouldn't be in the clubhouse, hmm? Now how did you know that?'

'Because I – I – ' She colored guiltily. 'All right, Roy, I saw her. I was snooping. But – it's not like you think! I was just curious about her, wondering why she'd come to Los Angeles. And she was always so nasty to me! I knew she was knocking me to you every chance she got. So I just thought who is she to be so high and mighty, and I talked with a friend of mine in Baltimore and – and – '

'I see. You must have some very knowledgeable friends.'

'Roy,' she begged. 'Don't be angry with me. I wouldn't do anything to hurt her any more than I would you.'

'You'd better never try,' he said. 'Lilly travels in some very fast company.'

'I know,' she nodded meekly. 'I'm sorry, dear.'

'Lilly didn't see you today?'

'Oh, no. I didn't hang around, Roy. Honest.' She kissed him, smiling into his eyes. 'Now, about us . . .'

'Yes,' he nodded. 'We may as well go back to Los Angeles, hadn't we? You've found out what you wanted to know.'

'Now, honey. Don't take it like that. I think I must have known for a long time. I was just waiting for the right opportunity to talk to you.'

'And just what do you know about me, anyway?'

'I know you're a short-con operator. A very good one, apparently.'

'You talk the lingo. What's your pitch?'

'The long end. The big-con.'

He nodded; waited. She snuggled close to him, pressing his hand against her breast. 'We'd make a hell of a team, Roy. We think alike; we get along well together. Why, darling, we could work for two months out of the year and live high for the other ten! I – '

'Wait,' he said, gently pushing her away. 'This isn't something to rush into, Moira. It's going to take a lot of talking about.'

'Well? So let's talk.'

'Not here. We didn't come here on business. We don't talk it here.'

She searched his face, and her smile faded a little. 'I see,' she said. 'You think it might be hard to give me a turndown here. It would be easier on the home grounds.'

'You're smart,' he said. 'Maybe you're too smart, Moira. But I didn't say I was turning it down.'

'Well . . .' She shrugged and stood up. 'If that's the way you want it . . .'

'That's the way I want it,' he said.

20

They caught the six o'clock train back to Los Angeles. It was crowded, as the train coming down had been, but the composition of the crowd was different. These passengers were largely business people, men who had put in a long day in San Diego and were now returning to their Los Angeles homes, or those who lived in San Diego and were due in Los Angeles early in the morning. Then, there were those few who had overstayed their weekends, and faced reproaches – or worse – when they arrived in the California metropolis.

The holiday spirit was definitely absent. A kind of moodiness pervaded the train, and some of it enveloped Moira and Roy.

They had a drink in the half-empty lounge. Then, discovering that the train carried no diner, they remained in the car for the rest of their ride. Seated in the cozy closeness of a booth, her thigh pressed warmly against his, Moira looked out at the aching loneliness of the sea, the naked and hungering hills, the houses closed firmly to all but themselves. The idea that she had propounded to him, something that was merely desired, became a tigerish must – a thing that had to be. It was either that or nothing, and so it had to be that.

She could not go on as she had the past few years, eking out her capital with her body, exchanging her body's use for the sustenance it needed. There were not enough years left, and the body inevitably used more than it received. Always, as the years grew fewer, the more rapidly the flesh depleted itself. So, an end to things as they had been. An end to the race with self. The mind grew youthful with use, increasingly eager with the demands of its owner, anxious and able to provide for the body that gave it shelter, to imbue it with its own youth and vigor or a reasonable facsimile thereof. And thus the mind must be used from now on. The ever-lucrative schemes which the mind could concoct and put into practice. Her mind and Roy's, the two working together as one, and the money which he could and must supply.

Perhaps she had pushed her hand a little too hard; no man liked to be pushed. Perhaps her interest in Lilly Dillon had been a blunder; every man was sensitive about his mother. But no matter. What she suggested was right and reasonable. It would be good for both of them.

It was what had to be. And damn him, he'd better – !

He made some casual comment, nudging her for a response, and seething with her own thoughts she turned on him, her face aged with hatred. Startled, he drew back frowning.

'Hey, now! What's the matter?'

'Nothing. Just thinking about something.' She smiled, dropping the mask so swiftly that he was not sure of what he had seen. 'What was it you said?'

He shook his head; he couldn't remember what it was now. 'But maybe I should know your name, lady. Your right one.'

'How about Langley?'

'Langley . . .' He puzzled over it for a moment. Then, '*Langley!* You mean, The Farmer? You teamed with Farmer Langley?'

'That's me, pal.'

'Well, now . . .' He hesitated. 'What happened to him, anyway? I heard a lot of stories, but – '

'The same thing that happens to all of 'em, a lot of them I mean. He just blew up; booze, dope, the route.'

'I see,' he said. 'I see.'

'Now, don't you worry about him.' She snuggled closer to him, misreading his attitude. 'That's all over and done with. There's just us now, Moira Langtry and Roy Dillon.'

'He's still alive, isn't he?'

'Possibly. I really don't know,' she said.

And she might have said, *And I don't care.* For the knowledge had come to her suddenly, though unsurprisingly, that she didn't care, that she had never really cared about him. It was as though she had been hypnotized by him, overwhelmed by his personality as others had been; forced to go his way, to accept his as the right and only way. Yet always subconsciously resisting and resisting, slowly building up hatred for being forced into a life – and what kind of life was it, anyway, for an attractive young woman? – that was entirely foreign to the one she wanted.

It was nothing clear, defined. Nothing she was consciously aware of or could admit to. But still she knew, in her secret mind, knew and felt guilty about it. And so, when the blowup came, she had tried to take care of him. But even that had been a means of striking back at him, the final firm push over the brink, and subconsciously knowing this she had felt still more guilty and was haunted by him.

Yet now, her feelings brought to the surface, she saw there was not and had never been anything to feel guilty about.

The Farmer had got what he deserved. Anyone who deprived her of something she wanted deserved what he got.

It was nine-fifteen when the train pulled into Los Angeles. She and Roy had a good dinner in the station restaurant. Then they ran through a light rain to his car, and drove out to her apartment.

She threw off her wraps briskly, turned to him holding out her arms. He held her for a moment, kissing her, but inwardly drawing back a little, subtly cautioned by something in her manner.

'Now,' she said, drawing him down onto the lounge, 'Now, we get down to business.'

'Do we?' He laughed awkwardly. 'Before we do that, maybe we'd better – '

'I can scrape up ten grand without much trouble. That would leave twenty or twenty-five for your end. There's a place in Oklahoma now, wide open if the ice is right. As good as Fort Worth was in the old days. We can move in there with a wire store, and – '

'Wait,' said Roy. 'Hold it, keed!'

'It would be perfect, Roy! Say, ten grand for the store, ten for the ice, and another ten for – '

'I said to hold it! Not so fast,' he said, angering a little now. 'I haven't said I was going to throw in with you.'

'What?' She looked at him blankly, a slight glaze over her eyes. 'What did you say?'

He repeated the statement, softening it with a laugh. 'You're talking some tall figures. What makes you think I've got that kind of money?'

'Why, you must have! You're bound to!' She smiled at

him firmly; a teacher reproving an errant child. 'Now, you know you do, Roy.'

'Do I?'

'Yes. I watched you work on the train, as slick an operator as I ever saw. You don't get that smooth overnight. It takes years, and you've been getting away with it for years. Living on a Square John income and taking the fools for – '

'And I've been doing some taking myself. Twice in less than two months. Enough to put me in the hospital here, and in San Diego today – '

'So what?' She brushed the interruption aside. 'That doesn't change anything. All it proves is that it's time you moved up. Get up where there's big dough at stake and you don't have to stick your neck out every day.'

'Maybe I like it where I am.'

'Well, I don't like it! What are you trying to pull on me, anyway? What the hell are you trying to hand me?'

He stared at her, not knowing whether to laugh or be angry, his lips twitching uncertainly. He had never seen this woman before. He had never heard her before.

The rain whispered against the window. Distantly, there was a faint whirring of an elevator. And with it, with those sounds, the sound of her heavy breathing. Labored, furious.

'I'd better run along now,' he said. 'We'll talk about it some other time.'

'We'll talk about it now, by God!'

'Then,' he said quietly, 'there's nothing to talk about, Moira. The answer is no.'

He stood up. She jumped up with him.

'Why?' she demanded. 'Just tell me why, damn you!'

Roy nodded, a glint coming into his eyes. He said that the best reason he could think of was that she scared the hell out of him. 'I've seen people like you before, baby. Double-tough and sharp as a tack, and they get what they want or else. But they don't get by with it forever.'

'Bull!'

'Huh-uh, history. Sooner or later the lightning hits 'em, honey. I don't want to be around when it hits you.'

He started for the door. Wild-eyed, her face mottled with rage, she flung herself in front of him.

'It's your mother, isn't it? Sure, it is! One of those keep-it-in-the-family deals! That's why you act so funny around each other! That's why you were living at her apartment!'

'Wh-aat?' He came to a dead stop. 'What are you saying?'

'Don't act so goddamned innocent! You and your own mother, *gah*! I'm wise to you, I should have seen it before! Why, you rotten son-of-a-bitch! How is it, hmm? How do you like – '

'How do you like this?' Roy said.

He slapped her suddenly, catching her with a backhanded slap as she reeled. She leaped at him, hands clawed, and he grabbed her by the hair and flung her, and she came down sprawling on the floor.

A little wonderingly he looked at her, as she raised her smudged and reddened face. 'You see?' he said. 'You see why it wouldn't do, Moira?'

'You d-dirty bastard! *You're* going to see something!'

'I'm sorry, Moira,' he said. 'Good night and good luck?'

21

At the curb outside her apartment house, he lingered briefly before entering his car; relishing the rain against his face, liking the cool, clean feel of it. Here was normality, something elemental and honest. He was very glad he was out here in the rain instead of up there with her.

Back at his hotel, he lay awake for a time, thinking about Moira; wondering at how little sense of loss he felt at losing her.

Was tonight merely a finalizing of something that he had long intended to do? It seemed so; it had the feeling about it of the expected. It might even be that his strong attraction for Carol had been a reaction to Moira, an attempt to attach himself to another woman and thus be detached from her.

Carol . . .

He fidgeted uncomfortably, then put her out of his mind. He'd have to do something about her, he decided. Some day soon, somehow, he'd have to smooth things over with her.

As for Moira . . .

He frowned, on the point of falling asleep, then relaxed with a shake of his head. No, no danger there. She'd gotten sore and blown her top, but she was probably regretting it already. At any rate, there was nothing she could do and she was too smart to try. Her own position was too tenuous. She was wide open for a smacking-down herself.

He fell into a deep sleep. Having slept so little the night before, he rested well. And it was after nine when he awakened.

He sprang out of bed, feeling good and full of energy, starting to plan the day's schedule as he reached for a robe. Then slowly, drearily, he sat back down. For here he was again as he had been last week. Here he was again, still, confronted by emptiness. Barred from his selling job, barred from any activity. Faced with a day, an endless series of days, with nothing to do.

Dully, he cursed Kaggs.

He cursed himself.

Again, hopefully hopeless, as he bathed and shaved, as he dressed and went out to breakfast, he sought some way out of the impasse. And his mind came up with the same two answers – answers which were wholly unacceptable.

One: He could take the sales manager's job – take it without further stalling around – and give up the grifting. Or, two: He could jump town and go to another city; begin all over again as he had begun when he first came to Los Angeles.

Breakfast over, he got into his car and began to drive, aimlessly, without destination; the most tiresome way of driving. When this became unbearable, as it very shortly did, he pulled in to the curb and parked.

Peevishly, his mind returned to the impossible problem.

Kaggs, he thought bitterly. That damned Perk (for Percival) Kaggs! *Why couldn't he have left me alone? Why did he have to be so damned sure that I —*

The futile thinking interrupted itself. His frown faded, and a slow smile played around his lips.

Kaggs was a man of snap judgment, a man who made up his mind in a hurry. So probably he would unmake it just as fast. He would take no nonsense from anyone. Given sufficient reason, and without apology, he would snatch back from the sales manager's job as promptly as he had proffered.

Roy called him from a nearby drugstore. He was still forbidden to work for a while (the doctor's orders), he said, but perhaps Kaggs would like to have lunch with him? Kaggs said that he seldom took time for lunch; he usually settled for a sandwich in his office.

'Maybe you should start going out,' Roy told him.

'Oh? You mean on account of my ulcers? Well – '

'I mean on account of your disposition. It might help you to get along better with people.'

He grinned coldly, listening to the startled silence that poured over the wire. Then, Kaggs said equably, 'Well, maybe it would at that. Twelve o'clock suit you?'

'No, it doesn't. I'd rather eat at one.'

Kaggs said, fine, that was better for him, too. 'One o'clock then. The little place across the street.'

Roy hung up the phone. He considered the advisability of showing up late for the appointment, and decided against it. That would be simply rudeness, crudeness. It would do nothing but arouse Kaggs' suspicions.

Already, perhaps, he had pursued the line of brusqueness too far.

He arrived at the restaurant a little before one.

They ate at a small table in the rear of the place, and somehow the meeting went pretty much as the first one had. Somehow, and much to Roy's annoyance, the feeling of empathy grew between them. Toward the end of the meal, Kaggs did a surprising thing – surprising, that is, for him. Reaching across the table, he gave Roy a shy slap on the shoulder.

'Feeling lousy, aren't you, boy? Like you could bite nails.'

'What?' Roy looked at him startled. 'What makes you think that?'

'You'd just have to; I know I would. A man can idle around so long, and then it begins to drive him nuts. Why don't you come back to the office with me for a while? Sort of look the setup over.'

'Well, I – you're busy, and – '

'So I'll put you to work, too.' Kaggs stood up, smiling. 'I'm kidding, of course. You can just look around; take a gander at the salesmen's file, if you like. Do what you want to, and pull out when you want to.'

'Well . . .' Roy shrugged. 'Why not?'

The question was rhetorical; he could think of no valid reason to decline. Similarly, finding himself in Kaggs' office at Sarber & Webb, he was forced to accept the file which Kaggs shoved in front of him. To show at least a semblance of interest in its various cards.

Resentfully, he saw himself a victim of Kaggs' highhandedness. Kaggs had taken charge of him again, as he had on that first day. But that wasn't really true. More accurately, he was his own victim, his own slave. He had made personality a profession, created a career out of selling himself. And he could not stray far, or for long, from his self-made self.

He riffled through the cards, unseeing.

He began to see them, to read the meaning in them. They became people and money and life itself. And thoughtfully, one at a time, he took them out of the file and spread them out on the desk.

He picked up a pencil, reached for a lined pad of scratch paper . . .

As he worked, Kaggs gave him an occasional covert glance, and a smug smile tightened his thin lips. A couple of hours passed, and Kaggs arose and strolled over to his desk.

'How are you doing?'

'Sit down,' Roy said, and as the other man obeyed, 'I think this record system is all wrong, Perk. I don't want to tread on anyone's toes, whoever set it up, but – '

'Tread away. Nothing's sacred around here.'

'Well, it's misleading, a waste of time. Take this man here. His gross sales for the week are six hundred and fifty dollars. His commission, over in this column, totals eighty-one dollars. What's his percentage of the week's sales?'

'I'd have to figure it up. Roughly, eight per cent.'

'Not necessarily. Depending on what he sold, he might have some twenty-five per cent stuff in there. The point is, just what the hell was it that he sold? How much of it was practically loss-leader stuff, items that we have to sell in order to compete?'

Kaggs looked at him sharply; hesitated. 'Well, of course, there's his sales slips; that's what his commissions were figured from.'

'But where are the sales slips?'

'Accounting gets a copy, inventory gets a copy, and of course the customer gets one at the time of purchase.'

'Why does inventory need a copy? The stuff is checked off at the time it leaves the shop, isn't it? Or at least it could be. You've got some duplicate effort if it isn't. Where you need a copy is here in the salesman's file.'

'But –'

'Not in a file like this, of course. There isn't enough room. But it doesn't have to be like this. We don't have so many salesmen that we couldn't set up a separate file on each one, give each man a section in one of the filing cabinets.'

Kaggs scratched his head. 'Hmm,' he said. 'Well maybe.'

'It ought to be done, Perk. It just about has to be if you're going to have a clear picture of what's going on. Tie the sales slips to the salesmen, and you know which men are selling and which are running a milk route. Ordertakers. You know what items are moving and which need pushing, and which should be dropped entirely. Of course, you'll know all that eventually, anyway. But waiting can cost you a hell of a lot of money and –'

Roy broke off abruptly, suddenly abashed by his tone and his words. He shook his head, dismayed, like a man coming into wakefulness.

'Just listen to me,' he said. 'I come in here for the first time, and I start kicking your system to pieces.'

'So kick it some more. Kick the crap out of it!' Kaggs beamed at him. 'How are you feeling, anyway? Getting tired? Want to knock off for the day?'

'No, I'm okay. But –'

'Well, let's see, then.' Kaggs skidded his chair closer, and reached for a pencil. 'What would you say to . . .'

An hour went by.

Two hours.

In the outer offices, one of the clerks turned a startled stare on her neighbor. 'Did you hear that?' she whispered. 'He was *laughing*! Old Picklepuss Kaggs laughed out loud!'

'I heard,' said the other girl, grimly, 'but I don't believe it. That guy never learned how to laugh!'

At five-thirty that evening, the telephone operator plugged in her night numbers and closed her board. The outer offices darkened and became silent, as the last of the office employees filed out. And at six, the downstairs workers departing to the muted clanging of the time-clock, the silence and the dimness became absolute.

At eight o'clock –

Perk Kaggs removed his glasses, and rubbed his eyes. He looked around, blinking absently, and a bewildered look spread over his face. With an amazed curse, he jumped to his feet.

'My God! Look at the time! Where the hell did the day go to?'

'What?' Roy frowned. 'What's the matter, Perk?'

'Come on, you're getting out of here! Right this minute, damnit! My God – ' Kaggs swore again. 'I ask you to drop in for a few minutes and you put in a day's work!'

They had a late dinner together.

As they said good night, Kaggs gave him a sharp searching glance. 'Level with me, Roy,' he said quietly. 'You do want this job, don't you? You want to be sales manager?'

'Well . . .' Roy hesitated for a flicker of a second.

There it was. Here was his chance to refuse. And he knew suddenly that he could refuse, without apology or explanation. He could say simply no, that he didn't want it, and that would be that. He could go back to his old life where he had left it. For something had happened between him and Kaggs, something that made them friends. And friends do not question each other's motives.

'Why, of course, I want it,' he said firmly. 'What gave you the idea that I didn't?'

'Nothing. I just thought that – nothing.' Kaggs returned to his usual briskness. 'To hell with it. To hell with you. Go home and get some sleep, and don't show up at the shop again until the doctor says you're ready!'

'You're the boss,' Roy grinned. ''Night, Perk.'

Driving back to the hotel, he started to rationalize his decision, to find some devious reason for doing what he had done. But that passed very quickly. Why shouldn't he take a job that he wanted to take? Why shouldn't a man want a friend, a real friend, when he has never before had one?

He put the car away and entered the hotel. The elderly night clerk hailed him.

'You had a phone call this morning, Mr Dillon. Your mother.'

'My mother?' Roy paused. 'Why didn't you leave word for me where I work?'

'I was going to, sir, but she said not to bother. Didn't have time to wait, I guess.'

Roy picked up a house phone, put in a call to Lilly's apartment. He hung up a moment or two later, puzzled, uneasy.

Lilly was gone. She had checked out of her apartment this morning, leaving no forwarding address.

He went upstairs. Frowning, he shucked out of his clothes and lay down on the bed. He tossed and turned for a while, worrying. Then, gradually, he relaxed and began to doze.

Lilly could take care of herself. There could be – must be – an innocent reason for her sudden move.

Del Mar . . . She might have moved there for the race meet. Or she might have found a more desirable apartment here in town that had to be taken immediately. Or perhaps Bobo Justus had suddenly recalled her to Baltimore.

He fell asleep.

After what seemed only an instant, he came awake.

Sunlight flooded the room. It was late in the morning. He was conscious that the phone had been ringing for a very long time. It was now silent, but its din was still in his ears. He started to reach for it, his senses dull, not fully free of the stupor of sleep, and there was a knock on the door, a steady knocking.

He crossed to it, opened it enough to look out. He blinked at the man there; then, the man identifying himself, stating his business with professional regret – apologizing for the errand that had brought him here – Roy let the door open wide.

And he stood shaking his head as the man came inside.

No, he shouted silently. It wasn't true! It was some stupid mistake! Lilly wouldn't be in Tucson! Why – why –

He said it aloud, glaring at his visitor. The latter pursed his lips thoughtfully.

'You didn't know she was in Arizona, Mr Dillon? She didn't tell you she was going?'

'Of course, she didn't! Because she didn't go! I – I – ' He hesitated, some of his caution asserting itself. 'I mean, my mother and I weren't very close. We went our own ways. I hadn't seen her for almost eight years until she came here a few weeks ago, but – '

'I understand,' the man nodded. 'That jibes with our information, such as it is.'

'Well, you're wrong, anyway,' Roy said doggedly. 'It's someone else. My mother wouldn't – '

'I'm afraid not, Mr Dillon. It was her own gun, registered to her. The proprietor of the tourist court remembers that she was very distraught. Of course, it does seem a little odd that she'd use a gun with a silencer on it for ... for something like that. But – '

'And she didn't! It doesn't make sense!'

'It never does, Mr Dillon. It never makes sense when a person commits suicide . . .'

22

The man was slightly bald, heavy-set, with a plump, honest face. His name was Chadwick, and he was a Treasury Department agent. Obviously, he felt a little awkward about being here at such a time. But it was his job, distasteful though it might be, and he meant to do it. He did, however, lead into his business circuitously.

'You understand why I came rather than the local police, Mr Dillon. It really isn't their affair, at least at this point. I'm afraid there may be some unpleasant publicity later on, when the circumstances of your mother's death are revealed. An attractive widow with so much money in her possession. But – '

'I see,' said Roy. 'The money.'

'More than a hundred and thirty thousand dollars, Mr Dillon. Hidden in the trunk of her car. I'm very much afraid – ' delicately. 'I'm afraid she hadn't paid taxes on it. She'd been falsifying her returns for years.'

Roy gave him a wry look. 'The body was discovered this morning; about eight o'clock, right? You seem to have been a very busy little man.'

Chadwick agreed simply that he had been. 'Our office here hasn't had time to make a thorough investigation, but the evidence is indisputable. Your mother couldn't have saved that much out of her reported income. She was a tax evader.'

'How terrible! Too bad you can't put her in jail.'

'Please!' Chadwick winced. 'I know how you feel, but – '

'I'm sorry,' Roy said quietly. 'That wasn't very fair. Just what do you want me to do, Mr Chadwick?'

'Well . . . I'm required to ask if you intend to lay claim to the money. If you care to say, that is. Possibly you'd rather consult a lawyer before you decide.'

'No,' Roy said. 'I won't lay any claim to the money. I don't need it, and I don't want it.'

'Thank you. Thank you, very much. Now, I wonder if you can give me any information as to the source of your mother's income. It seems obvious, you know, that there must have been tax evasions on the part of others, and – '

Roy shook his head. 'I imagine you know as much about my mother's associates as I do, Mr Chadwick. Probably,' he added, with a tiredly crooked grin, 'you know a hell of a lot more.'

Chadwick nodded gravely, and stood up. Hesitating, hat in hand, he glanced around the room. And there was approval in his eyes, and a quiet concern.

Lilly's money had had to be impounded, he murmured; her car, everything she owned. But Roy mustn't think that the government was heartless in these matters. Any sum necessary for her burial would be released.

'You'll want to see to the arrangements personally, I imagine. But if there's anything I can do to help . . .' He took a business card from his wallet and laid it on the table. 'If you can tell me when you might care to leave for Tucson, if you are going, that is, I'll notify the local authorities and – '

'I'd like to go now. Just as soon as I can get a plane.'

'Let me help you,' Chadwick said.

He picked up the phone, and called the airport. He spoke briskly, reciting a government code number. He glanced at Roy. 'Get you out in an hour, Mr Dillon. Or if that's too soon – '

'I'll make it. I'll be there,' Roy said, and he began flinging on his clothes.

Chadwick accompanied him to his car, shook hands with him warmly as Roy opened the door.

'Good luck to you, Mr Dillon. I wish we could have met under happier circumstances.'

'You've been fine,' Roy told him. 'And I'm glad we met, regardless.'

He had never seen the traffic worse than it was that day. It took all his concentration to get through it, and he was glad for the respite from thinking about Lilly. He got to the airport with ten minutes to spare. Picking up his ticket, he hurried toward the gate to his plane. And then, moved by a sudden hunch, he swerved into a telephone booth.

A minute or two later he emerged from it. Grim-faced, a cold rage in his heart, he went onto his plane. It was a propeller job since his trip was a relatively short one, a mere five hundred and eighty miles. As it circled the field and winged south, a stewardess began serving the pre-luncheon drinks. Roy took a double bourbon. Sipping it, he settled back in his seat and gazed out the window. But the drink was tasteless and he gazed at nothing.

Lilly. Poor Lilly . . .

She hadn't killed herself. She'd been murdered.

For Moira Langtry was also gone from her apartment. Moira also had checked out yesterday morning, leaving no forwarding address.

There was one thing about playing the angles. If you played them long enough, you knew the other guy's as well as you knew your own. Most of the time it was like you were looking out the same window. Given a certain set of circumstances, you knew just about what he would do or what he had done.

So, without actually knowing what had happened, just how and why Lilly had been brought to her death, Roy knew enough. He could make a guess which came astonishingly close to the truth.

Moira had a contact in Baltimore. Moira knew that Lilly would be carrying heavy – that, like any successful operator, she would have accumulated a great deal of money which would never be very far from her. As to just how far, just where it might be hidden, Moira didn't know. She might look forever without finding it. Thus Lilly had had to be put on the run; for, running, she would take the loot with her, necessarily narrowing its possible whereabouts to her immediate vicinity.

How to make her run? No problem there. For a fearful shadow lies constantly over the residents of Uneasy Street. It casts itself through the ostensibly friendly handshake, or the gorgeously wrapped package. It beams out from the baby's carriage, the barber's chair, the beauty parlor. Every neighbor is suspect, every outsider, everyone period; even one's own husband or wife or sweetheart. There is no ease on Uneasy Street. The longer one's tenancy, the more untenable it becomes.

You didn't need to frighten Lilly. Only to frighten her a little more. And if you had a contact at her home base, someone to give her a 'friendly warning' by telephone . . .

Roy finished his drink.

He ate the lunch which the stewardess served him.

She took the tray away and he smoked a cigarette, and the plane dropped lower over the desert and came into the Tucson glide pattern.

A police car was waiting for him at the airport. It carried him swiftly into the city, and a police captain took him into a private office and gave him such facts as he could.

'. . . checked into the motor court around ten last night, Mr Dillon. It's that big place with the two swimming pools; you passed it on the way into town. The night clerk says she seemed pretty jumpy, but I don't know that you can put much stock in that. People always remember that other people acted or looked or talked funny after something's happened to 'em. Anyway, your mother left a seven-thirty call, and when she didn't answer her phone one of the maids finally got around to looking in on her . . .'

Lilly was dead. She was lying in bed in her nightclothes. The gun was on the floor at the side of the bed. Judging by her appearance – *Roy winced* – she'd put the muzzle in her mouth and pulled the trigger.

There was no disarray in the room, no sign of a struggle, no suicide note. 'That's about all we know, Mr Dillon,' the captain concluded, and he added with casual pointedness, 'Unless you can tell us something.'

Roy said that he couldn't and that was true. He could

only say what he suspected, and such guilty suspicions would only damage him while proving nothing at all against Moira. It might make a little trouble for her, cause her to be picked up and questioned, but it would accomplish no more than that.

'I don't know what I could tell you,' he said. 'I've got an idea that she traveled with a pretty fast crowd, but I'm sure you're already aware of that.'

'Yes.'

'Do you think it might not have been suicide? That someone killed her?'

'No,' the captain frowned, hesitantly. 'I can't say that I think that. Not exactly. There's nothing to indicate murder. It does seem strange that she'd come all the way from Los Angeles to kill herself and that she'd get into her night-clothes before doing it, but, well, suicides do strange things. I'd say that she was badly frightened, so afraid of being killed that she went out of her mind.'

'That sounds reasonable,' Roy nodded. 'Do you think someone followed her to the motel? The person who'd frightened her, I mean.'

'Possibly. But the place is on the highway, you know. People are coming in and out at all hours. If the guilty person was one of them, it would be practically impossible to tab him, and short of getting his confession to making a death threat, I don't know how we could stick him if he was tabbed.'

Roy murmured agreement. There was only one thing more that he could say, one more little nudge toward Moira that he could safely give the captain.

'I'm sure you've already looked into it, captain, but what about fingerprints? Wouldn't they, uh – '

'Fingerprints,' the officer smiled sadly. 'Fingerprints are for detective stories, Mr Dillon. If you dusted this office, you'd probably have a hard time finding a clear set of mine. You'd probably find hundreds of smudged prints, and unless you knew when they were made and just who you were looking for, I don't know what the devil you'd do with them. Aside from that, criminals at work have an unfortunate habit of wearing gloves, and many of the worst ones have no police record. Your mother, for example, had never been mugged or printed. I'm sorry – ' he added quickly. 'I didn't mean to refer to her as a criminal. But . . .'

'I understand,' Roy said. 'It's all right.'

'Now, there are a few items of your mother's personal property which you'll want. Her wedding ring and so on. If you'll just sign this receipt . . .'

Roy signed, and was given a thin brown envelope. He pocketed it, the pitiful residue of Lilly's hard and harried years, and the captain escorted him back to the waiting police car.

The undertaking establishment was on a side street, a sedately imposing building of white stucco which blazed blindly in the afternoon sun. But inside it was almost sickeningly cool. Roy shivered slightly as he stepped into the too-fragrant interior; the manager of the place, apparently alerted to his coming, sprang forward sympathetically.

'So sorry, Mr Dillon. So terribly sorry. No matter how we try to prepare for these tragic moments – '

'I'm all right.' Roy removed his arm from the man's grasp. 'I'd like to see my mother's – my mother, please.'

'Shouldn't you sit down a moment first? Or perhaps you'd like a drink.'

'No,' Roy said firmly. 'I wouldn't.'

'It might be best, Mr Dillon. It would give us a little time to, uh ... Well, you understand, sir. Due to the unusual financial involvements, we have been unable to, uh, perform the cosmetic duties which we normally would. The loved one's remains – the poor dear face – '

Curtly, Roy cut him off. He understood, he said. Also, he said, enjoying the manager's wince of distaste, he knew what a bullet fired into a woman's mouth could do to her face.

'Now, I want to see her. Now!'

'As you wish, sir!' The man drew himself up. 'Please to follow me!'

He led the way to a white-tiled room behind the chapel.

The cold here was icy. A series of drawers was set into one of the frostily gleaming walls. He gripped a drawer by its metal handle and gave it a tug, and it glided outward on its bearings. With an offended gesture, he stepped back and Roy advanced to the crypt and looked into it.

He looked and looked quickly away.

He started to turn away. And then, slowly, concealing his surprise, he forced his eyes back on the woman in the coffin.

They were about the same size, the same coloring; they had the same full but delicately-boned bodies. But the hands! *The hand!* Where was the evil burn that had been inflicted on it, where was the scar that such a burn must leave?

Well, doubtless it was on the hand of the woman who had killed this woman. The woman whom Moira Langtry had intended to kill, and who had killed Moira Langtry instead.

23

It was late evening when the dusty Cadillac reached down-town Los Angeles; pulled up a few doors short of the Grosvenor-Carlton. The driver leaned wearily over the wheel for a moment, limp with exhaustion, a little dizzy from sleeplessness. Then, resolutely, she raised her head, removed the tinted sunglasses, and studied herself in the mirror.

Her eyes were strained, bloodshot, but that didn't matter. They would probably be a hell of a lot worse, she suspected, before she was safely out of this mess. The glasses covered them, also helping to disguise her face. With the glasses on, and with the scarf drawn tightly around her head and under her chin, she could pass as Moira Langtry. She'd done it back at the Tucson motel, and she could do it again.

She made some minor adjustments on the scarf, pulling it a little lower on her forehead. Then, throwing off her weariness, subjecting it to her will, she got out of the car and entered the hotel.

The clerk greeted her with the anxious smile of the aged. He heard her request, a command, rather, and a touch of uncertainty tinged his smile.

'Well, uh, Mr Dillon's out of town, Mrs Langtry. Went to Tucson this morning, and – '

'I know that, but he's due back in just a few minutes. I'm supposed to meet him here. Now, if you'll kindly give me his key . . .'

'But – but – you wouldn't like to wait down there?'

'No, I would not!' Imperiously she held out her hand. 'The key, please!'

Fumbling, he took the key from the rack and gave it to her. Looking after her, as she swung toward the elevator, he thought with non-bitterness that fear was the worst part of being old. The anxiety born of fear. A fella knew that he wasn't much good any more – oh, yes, he knew it. And he knew he didn't always talk too bright, and he couldn't really look nice no matter how hard he tried. So, knowing in his heart that it was impossible to please anyone, he struggled valiantly to please everyone. And thus he made mistakes, one after the other. Until, finally, he could no more bear himself than other people could bear him. And he died.

But maybe, he thought hopefully, this would be all right. After all, Mrs Langtry and Mr Dillon *were* good friends. And visitors did sometimes wait in a guest's room when the guest was out.

Meanwhile . . .

Entering Roy's room, the woman locked the door and sagged against it, briefly resting. Then, dropping the sun-glasses and her modishly large handbag on the bed, she went resolutely to the four box-framed clown pictures. They had caught her attention the first time she had seen them – something that struck a jarring note; entirely incompatible with the known tastes of their owner. They couldn't have been there as decoration, so they must serve another pur-pose. And without seeing the symbolism in the four wisely grinning faces; Clotho, Lachesis, Atropos, and a fourth self-nominated Fate, Roy Dillon – she had guessed what that purpose was.

Now, prying loose the backs of the pictures, she saw that her guess was right.

The money tumbled out, sheaf after sheaf of currency. Stuffing it into her bag, she was struck with unwilling admiration for Roy; he must be good to have piled up this much. Then, stifling this emotion, telling herself that the theft would be good for him by pointing up the fruitlessness of crime, she finished her task.

Large as it was, the bag bulged with its burden of loot. She could barely close the clasp, and she wasn't at all sure that it would stay closed.

She hefted it, frowning. She put it under her arm, draping an end of the stole over it, checked her appearance in the mirror. It didn't look bad, she thought. Not *too* bad. If only the damned thing didn't fly open as she was passing through the lobby! She considered the advisability of leaving some of the money behind, and abruptly vetoed the idea.

Huh-uh! She needed that dough. Every damned penny of it and a lot more besides.

She gave the mirror a final swift glance. Then, the purse clutched tightly under her arm, she crossed to the door and unlocked it, pulled it open. And fell back with a startled gasp.

'Hello, Lilly,' said Roy Dillon.

24

The basic details of her story were just about what Roy expected them to be . . .

First there had been the warning call from Baltimore; then, responding to it, her frantic, unreasoning flight. She drove as hard as she could and as long as she could. When she could go no further, she turned in at the Tucson tourist court.

The place had a garage, rather than individual car ports, and she hadn't liked that. But she was too tired to go farther; and since a garage attendant was on duty at all times, she could not reasonably object to the arrangement.

She put the loaded gun under her pillow. She undressed and went to bed. Yes, naturally she had locked her door, but that probably didn't mean much. Those places, motels and tourist courts, lost so many keys that they often had them made interchangeable, the same keys unlocking different doors. And that was doubtless the case here.

Anyway, she awakened hours later, with two hands clutching her throat. Hands that silenced any outcry she might make as they strangled her to death. She couldn't see who it was; she didn't care. She had been warned that she would be killed, and now she was being killed and that was enough to know.

She got the gun from under her pillow. Blindly, she had shoved it upward, into the face of her assailant. And pulled the trigger. And – and –

Lilly shuddered convulsively, her voice breaking. 'God, Roy, you don't know what it was like! What it means to kill someone! All your life you hear about it and read about it, b-but – but when you do it yourself . . .'

Moira was in her nightclothes, an old trick of nocturnal prowlers. Caught in another's room, they lay it to accident, claiming that they left their own room on some innocent errand and somehow strayed into the wrong one.

There was a tagged key in Moira's pocket – the key to a nearby room. Also, it was the key to Lilly's predicament. It pointed to a plan, ready-made, and without thinking she knew what she must do.

She put Moira in her bed. She wiped her own fingerprints from the gun, and pressed Moira's prints upon it. She spent the night in Moira's room, and in the morning she checked out under Moira's name and with the dead woman's clothes.

Naturally, she couldn't take her own car. The car and the money hidden in it now belonged to Moira also. For Moira was now Lillian Dillon, and Lilly was Moira Langtry. And so it must always be.

'What a mess! And all for nothing, I guess. I was jake with Bobo all the time, but now that it's happened . . .' She paused, brightening a little. 'Well, maybe it's a break for me, after all. I've been wanting out of the racket for years, and now I'm out. I can make a clean start, and – '

'You've already made a start,' Roy said. 'But it doesn't look very clean to me.'

'I'm sorry.' Lilly flushed guiltily. 'I hated to take your money, but – '

'Don't be sorry,' Roy said. 'You're not taking it.'

For a long moment, a silent second-long eternity, Lilly sat staring at her son. Looking into eyes that were her eyes, meeting a look as level as her own. So much alike, she thought, and the thought was also his. *Why can't I make him understand?* she thought. And he thought, *Why can't I make her understand?*

Shakily, a cold deadness growing in her heart, she arose and went into the bathroom. She bathed her face in the sink, patted it dry with a towel, and took a drink of water. Then, thoughtfully, she refilled the glass and carried it out to her son. Why, thank you, Lilly, he said, touched by the small courtesy, disarmed by it. And Lilly told herself, *He's asking for it. I helped him when he was in a bind, and if he tries to hold out on me now, well he just hadn't better.*

'I have to have that dough, Roy,' she said. 'She had a bankbook in her purse, but that doesn't do me any good. I can't risk tapping it. All she had on her was a few hundred bucks, and what the hell am I going to do with that?'

Roy said she could do quite a bit with it. A few hundred would get her to San Francisco or some other not-too-distant city. It would give her a month to live quietly while she looked for a job.

'A job!' Lilly gasped. 'I'm almost forty years old, and I've never held a legit job in my life!'

'You can do it,' Roy said. 'You're smart and attractive. There are any number of jobs you can hold. Just dump the Cad somewhere. Bury it. A Cad won't fit in with the way you'll be living, and – '

'Save it!' Lilly cut him off with an angry, knifing gesture. 'You sit there telling me what to do – a guy so crooked that he has to eat soup with a corkscrew – !'

'I shouldn't have to tell you. You should be able to see it for yourself.' Roy leaned forward, pleadingly. 'A legit job and a quiet life are the only way for you, Lil. You start showing up at the tracks or the hot spots and Bobo's boys will be on you.'

'I know that, damnit! I know I've got to lay low, and I will. But the other – '

'It's good advice, Lilly. I'm following it myself.'

'Yeah, sure you are! I see you giving up the grift!'

'What's so strange about it? It's what you wanted. You kept pushing it at me.'

'Okay,' Lilly said. 'So you're on the level. So you don't need the money, do you? You don't need it or want it. So why the hell won't you give it to me?'

Roy sighed; tried to explain why: to explain acceptably the most difficult of propositions; i.e., that the painful thing you are doing for a person is really for his or her own good. And yet, talking to her, watching her distress, there was in his mind, unadmitted, an almost sadistic exulting. *Harking back to childhood, perhaps, rooted back there, back in the time when he had known need or desire, and been denied because the denial was good for him.* Now it was his turn. Now he could do the right thing – and yes, it was right – simply by doing nothing. *Now now now the pimp disciplining his whore listening to her pleas and striking yet another blow. Now now now he was the wise and strong husband taking his frivolous wife in hand. Now now now his subconscious was taking note of the bond between them, the lewd, forbidden and until now unadmitted bond. And so he must protect her. Keep her from the danger which the money would inevitably lead her to. Keep her available . . .*

'Now, look, Lilly,' he said reasonably. 'That money wouldn't last you forever; maybe seven or eight years. What would you do then?'

'Well . . . I'd think of something. Don't worry about that part.'

Roy nodded evenly. 'Yes,' he said, 'you'd think of something. Another racket. Another Bobo Justus to slap you around and burn holes in your hand. That's the way it would turn out, Lilly; that way or worse. If you can't change now, while you're still relatively young, how could you do it when you were crowding fifty?'

Fifty? There was an ancient sound about it and the odor of haggishness and the mouse-mouthed look of death . . .

And Carol? Ah, yes, Carol. A dear girl, a desirable girl. Perhaps, except for the until-now-unadmitted bond, THE girl. But as it was, only a ploy, a pawn in the game of life, death – and love – between Roy and Lillian Dillon. So –

'So that's how it is, Lil,' Roy said. 'Why I can't let you have the money. I mean, uh – '

His voice faltered weakly, his eyes straying away from hers.

After a moment, Lilly nodded. 'I know what you mean,' she said. 'I think I know.'

'Well – ' he gestured, his hands suddenly awkward. 'It's certainly simple enough.'

'Yes,' Lilly said. 'It's simple enough. Very simple. And it's something else, too.'

There was a peculiar glow in her eyes, a strange tightness to her face, a subdued huskiness to her voice. Watching him, studying him, she slowly crossed one leg over the other.

'We're criminals, Roy. Let's face it . . .'

'We don't have to be, Lil. I'm turning over a new leaf. So can you.'

'But we've always had class. We've kept our private lives fairly straight. There's been certain things we wouldn't do . . .'

'I know! So there's no complications! I can – we can – '

The leg was swinging gently; hinting, speaking to him. Holding him hypnotized.

'Roy . . . what if I told you I wasn't really your mother? That we weren't related?'

'Huh!' He looked up startled. 'Why, I – '

'You'd like that, wouldn't you? Of course you would. You don't need to tell me. Now, why would you like it, Roy?'

He gulped painfully, attempted a laugh of assumed nonchalance. Everything was getting out of hand, out of his hands and into hers. The sudden awareness of his feelings, the sudden understanding of himself, all the terror and the joy and the desire held him thralled and wordless.

'Roy . . .' So softly that he could hardly hear it.

'Y-Yes?' *He gulped again.* 'Yes?'

'I want that money, Roy. I've got to have it. Now, what do I have to do to get it?'

Lilly, he said, or tried to say it, and perhaps he did say some of what he meant to. 'Lilly, you know you can't go on like you were; you know you'll be caught, killed. You know I'm only trying to help you. If you didn't mean so much to me, I'd let you have the damned money. But I've got to stop you. I – I – '

'Maybe – ' she was going to be fair about this. 'You mean you really won't give it to me, Roy? You won't? Or will you? Can't I change your mind? What can I do to get it?'

And how could he tell her? How say the unsayable? And yet, as she arose, moved toward him with the tempting grace with which Moira had used to move – *Moira, another older woman, who had in essence been Lilly* – he tried to tell her. And jumbled as it was, it was enough for Lilly.

Why don't you finish your water, dear? she said. And gratefully, welcoming this brief respite, he raised the glass. And Lilly, her grip tight on the heavy purse, swung it with all her might.

It's my fault, she told herself; the way I raised him, his age, my age, wrestling and brawling him as though he were a kid brother; my fault, my creation. But what the hell can I do about that, now?

The purse crashed against the glass, shattering it. The purse flew open, and the money spewed out in a green torrent. A torrent splattered and splashed with red.

Lilly looked at it bewilderedly. She looked at the gushing wound in her son's throat. He rose up out of his chair, clutching at it, and an ugly shard of glass oozed out between his fingers. He said bubblingly, 'Lil, I – w-whyy – ' and then his knees crumpled under him, and he doubled over and pitched down upon the carpet of red-stained bills.

It was over that quickly. Over before she could explain or apologize – insofar as there was anything to explain or apologize for.

Matter-of-factly, she began to toe the unstained money to one side, gathering the bills into a pile. She tied them up in a towel from the bathroom, stowed it inside her clothes, and took a final look around the room.

All clear, it looked like. Her son had been killed by Moira, by someone who didn't exist. Sure, her own finger-prints were all over the room, but that wouldn't mean anything. After all, she'd been a visitor to Roy's room before his death, and, anyway, Lilly Dillon was officially dead.

And maybe I am, she thought. Maybe I wish to God that I was!

Bracing herself, she let her eyes stray down to her son. Abruptly, a great sob tore through her body, and she wept uncontrollably.

That passed.

She laughed, gave the thing on the floor an almost jeering glance.

'Well, kid, it's only one throat, huh?'

And then she went out of the room and the hotel, and out into the City of Angels.